California Diaries #12

Sunny

Diary Three

Ann M. Martin

SCHOLASTIC INC.
New York Toronto London Auckland Sydney
Mexico City New Delhi Hong Kong

For Jean Feiwel,
who was there at the beginning
and who is always there.

No part of this publication may be reproduced in whole or in part, or stored in a retrieval system, or transmitted in any form or by any means, electronic, mechanical, photocopying, recording, or otherwise, without written permission of the publisher. For information regarding permission, write to Scholastic Inc., Attention: Permissions Department, 555 Broadway, New York, NY 10012.

ISBN 0-590-02390-X

12 11 10 9 8 7 6 5 4 3 2 1   9/9 0 1 2 3 4/0

Printed in the U.S.A.   40

First Scholastic printing, August 1999

TUESDAY 3/16
5:32 A.M.

I WONDER IF I'LL EVER BE ABLE TO SLEEP LATE AGAIN. MY INNER CLOCK IS ALL MESSED UP. I COULD FALL ASLEEP IN THE MIDDLE OF THE DAY, AND I COULD BE WIDE-AWAKE AT 4:00 A.M. I NEVER NEED TO SET AN ALARM CLOCK ANYMORE. NO MATTER WHAT TIME I SET IT FOR I ALWAYS WAKE UP BEFORE IT GOES OFF.

I CAN'T STOP THINKING ABOUT MOM. ALL DAY, ALL NIGHT. IS THIS WHAT'S CALLED AN OBSESSION?

6:03 A.M.

AFTER I WROTE THAT, I TRIED TO GO BACK TO SLEEP. PUT THE DIARY AWAY, TURNED OFF MY LIGHT, CRAWLED UNDER THE COVERS.

NO GOOD.

NADA.

FIRST ALL THESE THOUGHTS JUST KEPT BLOWING THROUGH MY BRAIN. THEN I COULD HEAR MOM DOWNSTAIRS CALLING TO DAD. IT WAS LIKE SOME MESSED-UP, BLURRY, NOT-QUITE-RIGHT SCENE

FROM MY CHILDHOOD. I THOUGHT BACK TO NIGHTS WHEN I WAS LITTLE AND SICK WITH THE FLU OR A COLD OR SOMETHING. I COULDN'T SLEEP AND I'D CALL OUT AND IN A FLASH MOM WOULD BE THERE FOR ME. NOW I LIE IN MY BED AND LISTEN TO MOM CALL OUT. EVERYTHING IS WRONG WITH THIS SCENE. MOM IS IN BED DOWNSTAIRS, NOT UPSTAIRS IN HER OWN ROOM, THE ROOM SHE SHOULD BE SHARING WITH DAD. AND SHE, THE ADULT, IS THE ONE CALLING OUT, WHILE DAD IS THE ONE RUSHING TO COMFORT HER.

GOD, I CAN'T STAND IT.

MAYBE I'LL GO TO SCHOOL TODAY.

6:24 A.M.

I CAN'T DECIDE. SHOULD I GO TO SCHOOL TODAY? I DON'T WANT TO BE THERE, OF ALL PLACES, IF MOM SHOULD

LET ME START OVER. I MEAN, IF MOM

THIS IS TOO HARD.

6:45 A.M.

Okay, I'm going to go to school. I'm driving myself crazy here.

We're keeping a vigil.

A <u>vigil</u>. Who keeps watch these days? That sounds archaic. But that's what I overheard Dad say on the phone last night. He was talking (whispering, really) to someone from the bookstore. He said that yes, Mom had come home from the hospital a few days ago and we're keeping a vigil. Sometimes, especially lately, Dad seems overly dramatic to me, so I take the vigil reference with a grain of salt.

God.

I'm being driven crazy.

Even this journal is driving me crazy. Sometimes it feels like my only true friend. At the same time I feel as though I'm chained to it (emotionally).

All right. That's it. I'm going to go to school today. Dad will call me if anything changes.

9:40 A.M.

WHAT A MISTAKE. I SHOULDN'T HAVE COME
HERE. I CAN'T CONCENTRATE. I HAVEN'T EVEN BEEN
TO CLASS YET. I FEEL LIKE EVERYONE'S STARING AT
ME. THE ONES WHO KNOW ME WELL ARE THINKING,
"THERE SHE IS. POOR SUNNY." THE ONES WHO
DON'T KNOW ME WELL ARE THINKING, "IS THAT
HER? IS SHE THE ONE WHOSE MOTHER IS DYING?"

MOM IS DYING KIND OF DRAMATICALLY. MAYBE
THAT'S WHY DAD SEEMS SO DRAMATIC THESE DAYS.
THIS IS LIKE NOTHING YOU EVER HEAR ABOUT IN
REAL LIFE. I THOUGHT PEOPLE ONLY DIED THIS WAY
IN THE MOVIES. LIKE BETH IN LITTLE WOMEN.
JUST MADE-UP PEOPLE. I THOUGHT WHEN REAL
PEOPLE DIED YOU SAT AROUND IN THE HOSPITAL
WAITING ROOM UNTIL FINALLY THE DOCTOR CAME OUT
AND SAID, "WELL, IT'S OVER." AND THEN EVERYONE
CRIED AND STARTED TO MAKE FUNERAL
ARRANGEMENTS.

MY HEAD IS SWIMMING.

TIRED. NO SLEEP.

VERY MAD.

STILL HAVEN'T BEEN TO CLASS. NOT EVEN SURE WHAT PERIOD THIS IS.

FIRST I SAT IN THE LIBRARY. THEN IT STARTED TO FILL UP. MOVED TO AN EMPTY CLASSROOM. A CLASS CAME IN. MOVED TO A SPOT OUTSIDE THE FRONT DOORWAY.

WARM TODAY.

A MILLION TEACHERS HAVE SEEN ME AND NOT ONE HAS SAID ANYTHING. I MEAN, SAID ANYTHING TO ME ABOUT NOT BEING IN CLASS. MR. HACKETT SAID, "HOW'S IT GOING, SUNNY?" LIKE HE WAS ASKING ABOUT A SOCIAL STUDIES PROJECT, AND I SAID, "FINE."

10:50 A.M.

STILL SITTING OUT HERE. NO ONE IS BOTHERING ME.

I THINK I CAN SMELL THE OCEAN.

ONCE, WHEN I WAS FIVE, I WAS INVITED TO A BIRTHDAY PARTY. SOME KID IN MY KINDERGARTEN CLASS WAS TURNING SIX. I DIDN'T WANT TO GO. I KNEW WE WERE GOING TO PLAY PIN-THE-TAIL-ON-

THE-DONKEY, AND I HATED THAT GAME. I HATED
BEING BLINDFOLDED AND SPUN AROUND. IT WAS
EMBARRASSING AND HUMILIATING, EVERYONE WATCHING
YOU DUMBLY LOOK FOR THE DONKEY, THE STUPID
CARDBOARD TAIL CLUTCHED IN YOUR HAND. AND FOR
WHAT? SO YOU COULD WIN A SET OF MARKERS OR
A PLASTIC CHARM BRACELET? I TOLD MOM I
DIDN'T WANT TO GO TO THE PARTY AND SHE MADE
ME GO ANYWAY.

    I TOLD HER I HATED HER.

11:11 A.M.

    YOU KNOW, THIS IS KIND OF NICE. I'M STILL
SITTING BY THE DOOR. JUST ME AND MY
NOTEBOOK. THAT'S IT. NO BOOKS, NO WALKMAN.
DON'T EVEN HAVE MY PURSE. I STUCK SOME
CHANGE IN MY PANTS POCKET THIS MORNING,
GRABBED THE JOURNAL, AND LEFT.

11:13 A.M.

    I DIDN'T SAY GOOD-BYE TO MOM.

11:25 A.M.

I FEEL LIKE I'M ALICE, DOWN THE RABBIT
HOLE. EVERYONE HERE IS LIVING IN A DIFFERENT
WORLD. I THINK I'M A VISITOR FROM SOME OTHER
PLACE. THE PEOPLE HERE — THEY WALK AROUND SO
EASILY. THEY DON'T KNOW HOW AWFUL LIFE CAN BE.
AND ME — I CAN'T ESCAPE FROM IT.

1:12 P.M.

DAWN FOUND ME AND SNAGGED ME AT
LUNCHTIME. SHE LOOKED KIND OF WARY OF ME, BUT
AT THE SAME TIME SHE INSISTED I GO TO THE
CAFETERIA WITH HER. I WAS EXPECTING THAT SHE
WOULD DRAG ME TO A TABLE WITH MAGGIE AND
AMALIA. BUT SHE LED ME TO AN EMPTY TABLE
AND WE SAT ALONE. I WASN'T GOING TO EAT
ANYTHING, BUT DAWN HANDED ME SOMETHING. A
WEEK OR SO AGO THIS WOULD HAVE DRIVEN ME
CRAZY. TODAY I DIDN'T MIND. I FEEL NUMB. I
ATE WHATEVER SHE GAVE ME. I'M NOT EVEN SURE
WHAT IT WAS. A SANDWICH?

SAW DUCKY IN THE HALL AFTER LUNCH. HE

ACTUALLY SHIED AWAY FROM ME. EVERYONE HAS BEEN KEEPING THEIR DISTANCE, BUT NOBODY ELSE IS DOING WHAT DUCKY DOES. THEN AGAIN, I HAVEN'T DONE TO ANYONE ELSE WHAT I DID TO DUCKY. I KNOW I WAS UNFAIR — REALLY UNFAIR — WHEN I CALLED HIM A WIMP, AND SAID HE NEVER STANDS UP FOR HIMSELF, AND BASICALLY THAT MOST KIDS THINK HE'S A TOTAL DWEEB. BUT I DON'T HAVE THE ENERGY TO WORK UP AN APOLOGY. NOT EVEN TO DUCKY.

1:22 P.M.

BACK IN MY SPOT. NOW THAT IT'S LATER IN THE DAY AND EVEN WARMER, A FEW KIDS WERE SITTING HERE WHEN I RETURNED. I SAT A LITTLE DISTANCE AWAY FROM THEM. AND THEY SCATTERED. I'M LIKE INSECT REPELLENT. VERY EFFECTIVE INSECT REPELLENT. THESE KIDS COULD TALK ABOUT ALMOST ANYTHING — DRUGS, DRINKING. AND THEY ACT SO COOL, SWAGGERING AROUND WITH THEIR CIGARETTES IN THEIR POCKETS. BUT BRING UP THE IDEA OF THEIR PARENTS DYING AND THEY CAN'T HANDLE IT. AND I'M THE REMINDER OF WHAT THEY DON'T WANT TO THINK ABOUT.

So they scattered.

And I'm alone again.

I remember this one time when Dawn, Maggie, and I — oh, and Jill. Jill was there too. Hard to believe. When was the last time I saw her outside of school? I wonder if she knows how bad it's become with Mom. Of course she does. Everybody knows. I live under a microscope and everyone is lining up waiting for a turn to squint into it and look at the poor odd creature exposed on the glass slide.

Anyway, Dawn, Maggie, Jill, and I were having a sleepover at my house and it was almost 4:00 in the morning and we still couldn't go to sleep. We couldn't even settle down. We were giggling hysterically in my room and finally Mom came in. We thought she was going to separate us or something, but instead she told us about this sleepover she had when she was our age. Told us about her friends and the boys they talked about.

Dawn always remembers that. She mentions it a lot.

Ms. Krueger found me. She sat with me for a few minutes. Ms. Krueger is cool, I guess. She said to me, "How are you doing, Sunny?" which isn't so different from "How's it going, Sunny?" But it felt entirely different. She said it with such warmth and sincerity.

I said, "It's really hard."

And she nodded. She didn't say, "Well, obviously," or anything. Then she took my hand. "Come to me anytime. You know where my office is. And here. Let me give you my home phone number." Which she did.

After she left I decided to go home. I felt all watery, like I was going to spill over.

But guess what. I didn't. Go home, I mean. Not yet. There I was, about ready to spill over, and suddenly I felt like lead. I just kept remembering all these things.

I remembered when Mom first got the diagnosis. It was so unexpected. We really didn't know anything was wrong with her. Mom had gone to the doctor for a regular checkup and the doctor had run all these tests, but

JUST ROUTINE TESTS. NO ONE WAS EVEN THINKING ABOUT THE DOCTOR OR THE CHECKUP WHEN THE PHONE RANG THAT DAY. WE WEREN'T SITTING AROUND WAITING FOR IT TO RING, WAITING TO HEAR NEWS OF SOME SORT.

AND SO IT WAS A PHONE CALL THAT CHANGED EVERYTHING; CHANGED OUR LIVES. THE DOCTOR SAID HE HAD NOTICED SOMETHING ABNORMAL IN HER LUNGS AND HE WANTED TO RUN MORE TESTS. I REMEMBER THAT MOM SAID, "BUT I FEEL FINE." EVEN SO, SHE HAD TO GO BACK TO THE DOCTOR, THEN TO THE HOSPITAL, AND EVER SINCE, MY LIFE HAS BEEN A PARADE OF HOSPITALS AND TREATMENTS AND WAITING ROOMS. I MEAN, MOM'S LIFE HAS BEEN.

GOD, IT'S HOT. WHEN DID IT GET SO HOT?

YOU KNOW WHAT? I HAVE TO GET OUT OF HERE.

2:13 P.M.

I COULDN'T STAY IN SCHOOL. I HAD TO LEAVE. IT WAS SO HOT IN THE SUN AND THE SUN MADE ME THINK OF SUNNY AND SUNNY MADE ME THINK OF SUNSHINE AND SUNSHINE MADE ME THINK OF HOW

MY NAME CAME FROM MY FATHER AND MY MOTHER. ALL THOUGHTS SEEM TO LEAD BACK TO MY MOTHER.

My BRAIN IS NO LONGER MY OWN. IT'S BEEN HIJACKED BY MOM.

I HATE YOU, MOM.

I LOVE YOU, MOM.

I'M SITTING ON THIS ROCK UNDER THIS TREE THAT IS HALFWAY BETWEEN OUR HOUSE AND VISTA. IN THIRD GRADE DAWN AND I ACTUALLY COUNTED THE STEPS FROM THE END OF MY DRIVEWAY TO THE FRONT STEPS OF THE SCHOOL. AND THE ROCK AND TREE ARE EXACTLY HALFWAY BETWEEN.

THIRD GRADE. THAT WAS A LIFETIME AGO. OR MAYBE IT WAS SOMEONE ELSE'S LIFE. DID I EVER GO TO THIRD GRADE? WAS I EVER SO YOUNG? I DON'T THINK SO. I'M OLD, OLD, OLD.

MY FRIENDS. DAWN, MAGGIE, AMALIA, DUCKY. THERE FOR ME. ESPECIALLY DAWN. EVER SINCE I MOVED NEXT DOOR TO HER. A LONG TIME AGO.

I DON'T WANT TO GO HOME. I DIDN'T WANT TO BE AT SCHOOL, BUT NOW I DON'T WANT TO

BE AT HOME. WAITING, WAITING, WAITING. THE
VIGIL.

I CUT THE END OF SCHOOL AND NOBODY SAID
A WORD. I WALKED OUT OF SCHOOL RIGHT UNDER
EVERYONE'S NOSE. IT WAS THE EASIEST CUT OF MY
LIFE.

I AM SO TIRED. WILL I EVER NOT BE TIRED?

I WONDER WHAT CANCER FEELS LIKE. I ASKED
MOM ONCE, BUT SHE DIDN'T HAVE AN ANSWER.

JUST NOW, I LOOKED AT MY WATCH. SCHOOL'S
OUT. ANY MINUTE, KIDS ARE GOING TO START
STREAMING PAST ME. I WONDER WHERE ELSE I CAN
GO. WHERE ELSE I CAN BE PRIVATE.

ALL RIGHT. I GIVE UP. I KNOW I SHOULD GO
HOME. I'M JUST KILLING TIME HERE, PUTTING OFF
HAVING TO SEE MOM AGAIN.
GOD, DID I REALLY WRITE THAT? I DID. I
JUST WROTE THAT I'M PUTTING OFF HAVING TO
SEE MOM AGAIN.
I AM A HORRIBLE PERSON.

I KNEW IT. I KNEW THAT IF I CAME HOME MY LIFE WOULD NO LONGER BE MY OWN. AND I WAS RIGHT.

AUNT MORGAN HAS ONLY BEEN HERE SINCE YESTERDAY AND ALREADY IT FEELS LIKE SHE LIVES HERE. SHE SAYS SHE'S JUST TRYING TO KEEP THE HOUSE IN ORDER. OKAY. FINE. KEEP THE HOUSE IN ORDER, AUNT MORGAN. BUT KEEP IT IN OUR ORDER, NOT YOURS.

AUNT MORGAN IS A CONTROL FREAK. HOW CAN SHE BE MOM'S SISTER? THE FIRST THING SHE SAID WHEN I WALKED THROUGH THE DOOR THIS AFTERNOON WAS, "SUNNY, YOU'RE NOT SORTING THE LAUNDRY PROPERLY."

YOU KNOW WHAT I SAY TO THAT? I SAY, "SCREW THE LAUNDRY." WHY IS SHE EVEN THINKING ABOUT LAUNDRY AT A TIME LIKE THIS? IT'S NOT AS IF WE DON'T HAVE OTHER CLOTHES TO WEAR. CONSIDERING WHAT'S GOING ON AT OUR HOUSE, WE COULD PROBABLY RUN AROUND NAKED AND NO ONE WOULD NOTICE.

A HORRIBLE THOUGHT: AUNT MORGAN IS NOT MARRIED, WHICH SHOULDN'T COME AS ANY SURPRISE. BUT WHAT IF AFTER MOM DIES, IN THE TURMOIL,

SHE AND DAD DECIDE THEY'RE ATTRACTED TO EACH OTHER, AND DAD ASKS AUNT MORGAN TO MARRY HIM AND SHE LEAVES ATLANTA AND BECOMES MY STEPMOTHER?

OH MY GOD. I CAN'T BELIEVE I JUST WROTE "AFTER MOM DIES."

3:35 P.M.

GRANDMA CALLED. SHE AND GRANDAD WANT TO COME BY. THEY USED TO JUST DROP BY. SINCE WHEN DO THEY CALL FIRST? DAD SAID TO HER, "NOW ISN'T A GOOD TIME." HE REALLY SAID THAT. TO HIS OWN MOTHER. WHEN IS IT GOING TO BE A GOOD TIME?

ALSO, COULDN'T DAD HAVE CONSULTED WITH ME? I LOVE MY GRANDPARENTS. MAYBE PARTLY BECAUSE THEY'RE THE ONLY TWO I HAVE LEFT? ANYWAY, I WISH THEY WOULD COME OVER. GRANDMA IS ALL SOFT AND POWDERY AND UNDERSTANDING. WHEN I WAS LITTLE I USED TO CALL HER UP AFTER SCHOOL ALMOST EVERY DAY TO TELL HER WHAT HAD GONE ON. I'D TELL HER EVERYTHING — WHAT I ATE FOR LUNCH, WHO HIT WHOM, WHAT DAWN AND I TALKED ABOUT ON THE WAY TO

SCHOOL, ANSWERS I GOT WRONG, ANSWERS I GOT RIGHT. I'D CHATTER AND CHATTER AWAY AND SHE WOULD MAKE LITTLE MURMURING NOISES. EVERY OTHER SATURDAY I WOULD SPEND THE NIGHT AT THEIR HOUSE. I FELT LIKE A PRINCESS. A VERY GROWN-UP PRINCESS.

WHEN I WAS SIX GRANDMA AND GRANDAD TOOK ME TO A FANCY RESTAURANT FOR DINNER. THEY LET ME ORDER SHRIMP COCKTAIL AND DIDN'T MIND AT ALL WHEN I DECIDED I DIDN'T LIKE IT. GRANDAD ATE IT INSTEAD. (I THINK HE KNEW I WASN'T GOING TO LIKE IT.)

GRANDMA AND GRANDAD LOVE ME ENOUGH TO LET ME MAKE MISTAKES.

SO DOES MOM.

I GUESS I SHOULD GO DOWNSTAIRS AND SEE MOM. SHE WAS ASLEEP WHEN I CAME HOME, BUT I KNOW SHE'S AWAKE NOW. I CAN HEAR DAD AND AUNT MORGAN GOING IN AND OUT OF HER ROOM.

MORE LATER.

4:04 P.M.

SAW MOM. WE TALKED A LITTLE. AUNT MORGAN GAVE US SPACE. DAD TRIED TO GIVE US

SPACE BUT KEPT INTERRUPTING. MOM NOT REALLY
AWAKE.

4:10 P.M.

WELL, THAT WAS STUPID. THAT LAST ENTRY, I
MEAN. I JUST REREAD IT. IT DOESN'T SAY
ANYTHING. I'M SO CONFUSED.

THIS DIARY IS MY FRIEND. IT IS MY
CONFIDANTE, EVEN MORE THAN DAWN IS. LIKE, I
ACTUALLY <u>COULDN'T</u> SAY JUST ANYTHING TO DAWN.
NOT SURE WHY. BUT I DO SAY ABSOLUTELY
EVERYTHING TO MY JOURNAL. OR AT LEAST I USED
TO. I DON'T THINK I'VE BEEN DOING THAT SO
MUCH ANYMORE. I FEEL CLOSED UP, LIKE A SEALED
BOTTLE. I NEED TO OPEN UP. OR TO BE OPENED
UP.

I'M GOING TO TRY THAT LAST ENTRY AGAIN.

OKAY. HERE GOES.

FOR STARTERS, DAD IS AT HOME (AS I SAID).
HE'S BEEN AT HOME FOR SEVERAL DAYS STRAIGHT.
HE'S PRETTY MUCH ABANDONED THE BOOKSTORE. HE

STAYS WITH MOM JUST ABOUT ROUND THE CLOCK. HE EVEN SLEEPS IN HER ROOM. AND OF COURSE A NURSE IS USUALLY HERE, AND ONE DOCTOR OR ANOTHER CHECKS IN ON HER EVERY DAY. WHEN I WENT DOWNSTAIRS, DAD WAS SITTING WITH MOM, AND A NURSE WAS JUST OUTSIDE THE ROOM. AUNT MORGAN WAS IN THE KITCHEN. IN OTHER WORDS, NO PRIVACY.

"HI," I SAID TO DAD. "CAN I TALK TO MOM?"

"SURE, HONEY." HE WAS SITTING ON THE END OF HER BED.

"MAYBE I COULD TALK TO HER ALONE?" I SAID THIS LIKE IT WAS A QUESTION.

"OH. OH, OF COURSE." DAD STOOD UP AND WALKED INTO THE LIVING ROOM. I COULD HEAR HIM TALKING TO THE NURSE IN A VERY LOW VOICE.

I SAT AT THE FOOT OF MOM'S HOSPITAL BED AND GAZED AT HER, TRYING TO FIGURE OUT IF SHE REALLY WAS AWAKE. IT'S HARD TO KNOW THESE DAYS. YOU CAN'T TELL BY HER EYES. SOMETIMES SHE'S AWAKE WITH HER EYES CLOSED. I THINK IT'S TOO MUCH EFFORT TO KEEP THEM OPEN FOR LONG PERIODS OF TIME.

"MOM?" I WHISPERED.

Mom's eyes fluttered open. "Hi, sweetie," she said.

"Hi."

"How was school?"

"Fine. How are you feeling?" I knew this was a dumb question, but I didn't know what else to say.

"About the same." Mom licked her lips.

"Do you want some water?"

"Just some ice. Please."

I brought Mom some ice chips and put a few of them in her mouth.

"Thanks," she said after a few moments. "That's better."

I didn't know what to say then and I was embarrassed. How could I not know what to say to Mom? To Mom?

While I was still trying to dredge up a little piece of conversation, Mom said, "You are a very strong person, Sunny."

I bit my lip. I don't feel strong.

"Maybe you don't feel that way," Mom went on as if she'd read my mind, "but it's true. You can survive anything."

Well, that didn't make any sense. Mom is

A STRONG PERSON TOO, AND SHE ISN'T GOING TO SURVIVE CANCER. "I DON'T KNOW," I SAID.

DAD POKED HIS HEAD INTO THE ROOM THEN. "CAN I GET YOU ANYTHING?" HE ASKED MOM.

MOM SHOOK HER HEAD. "NO, THANKS."

DAD JUST STOOD THERE IN THE DOORWAY, LOOKING AT MOM. I STARED AT HIM. FINALLY HE WENT AWAY.

AFTER DAD LEFT, MOM SAID, "SUNNY, WHEN I'M GONE —"

AND I GASPED. RIGHT OUT LOUD. I DON'T KNOW WHETHER MOM HEARD ME, BUT

HOW COULD SHE START A SENTENCE LIKE THAT?

"WHEN I'M GONE," MOM WAS SAYING, "YOU AND DAD TAKE CARE OF EACH OTHER, OKAY?"

"OKAY," I WHISPERED.

"YOU'RE GOING TO NEED EACH OTHER."

I NODDED. THEN I REALIZED MOM'S EYES WERE SHUT AGAIN AND SHE COULDN'T SEE ME NOD, SO I WHISPERED, "YES."

"YOU'LL HAVE GRANDMA AND GRANDAD, OF COURSE. AND DAWN. BUT YOU AND DAD — YOU'LL HAVE TO TAKE CARE OF EACH OTHER."

SOON DAD STUCK HIS HEAD IN THE ROOM AGAIN, AND I WONDERED IF HE'D BEEN LISTENING

AT THE DOOR. I FROWNED AT HIM. "DAD —" I
BEGAN TO SAY.

"OH, SORRY." HE PULLED HIS HEAD BACK LIKE A
TURTLE, AND THIS HUGE FEELING OF DISGUST
WASHED OVER ME.

I LOOKED AT MOM AGAIN. "MOM?"

NO ANSWER. SHE HAD FALLEN ASLEEP. SHE
DOES THAT A LOT THESE DAYS. SHE CAN FALL
ASLEEP IN THE MIDDLE OF TALKING TO YOU, RIGHT
IN THE MIDDLE OF A SENTENCE. SO I TIPTOED
OUT OF THE ROOM. I NEARLY RAN INTO DAD.

"WERE YOU EAVESDROPPING?" I ASKED.

DAD'S MOUTH DROPPED OPEN.

AND IN A FLASH, AUNT MORGAN APPEARED.
SHE'S LIKE AN EVIL WITCH IN A FAIRY TALE.
"SUNNY," SHE SAID IN A WARNING TONE.

I DIDN'T ANSWER HER. I PICTURED HER IN HER
BIG OFFICE IN ATLANTA, ORDERING HER ASSISTANTS
AND SECRETARIES AROUND. I BET SHE YELLS AT
PEOPLE.

DAD STEPPED IN. "IT'S ALL RIGHT, MORGAN,"
HE SAID.

I LET OUT A BREATH I'D BEEN HOLDING. I
KNEW WE WEREN'T GOING TO FIGHT. WE'VE BEEN
MUCH TOO SUBDUED FOR FIGHTING LATELY. WE
DON'T FIGHT. WE DON'T HUG. WE DON'T YELL. WE

DON'T HAVE LONG LATE-NIGHT CHATS. WE JUST
TIPTOE AROUND EACH OTHER. IT'S LIKE WE DON'T
HAVE THE ENERGY FOR A FIGHT. OR FOR ANY KIND
OF BIG EMOTION. ANY BIG EMOTION BETWEEN US,
I MEAN. I THINK WE'RE SAVING ALL THE BIG
EMOTION FOR MOM.

6:35 P.M.

IT'S ALMOST DINNERTIME, AND I'M DELAYING
GOING DOWNSTAIRS AND FACING DAD AND AUNT
MORGAN. I'M REREADING WHAT I WROTE A LITTLE
EARLIER.

I AM SO LAME. I AM SUCH A COWARD. EVEN
HERE IN MY JOURNAL I'M NOT BEING HONEST. I
LEFT OUT A WHOLE BIG IMPORTANT PART OF MY
CONVERSATION WITH MOM. I COULDN'T BEAR TO
WRITE IT DOWN.

BUT NOW I WILL.

AFTER MOM SAID DAD AND I WILL HAVE TO
TAKE CARE OF EACH OTHER, SHE SAID, "DO YOU
KNOW SOMETHING? SINCE THE MOMENT YOU WERE
BORN I HAVE BEEN LOOKING FORWARD TO YOUR
WEDDING DAY. ISN'T THAT SILLY? WHAT IF YOU

DON'T WANT TO GET MARRIED? LOTS OF PEOPLE
DON'T. BUT STILL, I'VE LOOKED FORWARD TO THAT
DAY. I'VE DREAMED OF YOU WEARING MY WEDDING
DRESS."

"MOM —"

"AND I WANT YOU TO KNOW WHERE IT IS."

"MOM —"

"IT'S IN A BOX IN THE ATTIC. THE BOX SAYS
WEDDING DRESS ON IT."

"OKAY."

AND THEN DAD STUCK HIS HEAD IN THE ROOM
AGAIN.

I DON'T UNDERSTAND. WHY DO PEOPLE HAVE
TO DIE? ALL RIGHT, THAT'S A STUPID QUESTION.
THEY HAVE TO DIE BECAUSE IF EVERYONE LIVED, AND
BABIES KEPT ON BEING BORN, THE WORLD WOULD
HAVE BECOME OVERCROWDED A LONG, LONG TIME
AGO.

OKAY, WHY DO GOOD, YOUNG PEOPLE HAVE TO
DIE? WHY DOES MOM HAVE TO DIE NOW? WHY
COULDN'T SHE DIE WHEN SHE'S REALLY, REALLY OLD,
THE WAY MOST PEOPLE DO?

I AM NOT READY FOR MOM TO DIE.
AND THERE'S NOT A THING I CAN DO
ABOUT IT.

THIS IS UNFAIR, UNFAIR, UNFAIR.
I DON'T WANT MOM TO LEAVE YET.

I GOT CALLED DOWN TO DINNER. WHEN AUNT MORGAN CALLS, YOU OBEY. ACTUALLY, I WAS KIND OF RELIEVED TO CLOSE UP THE JOURNAL AND DO SOMETHING MUNDANE, LIKE EAT.

AUNT MORGAN IS NOT MUCH OF A COOK. OR A HOUSEKEEPER. BUT SHE SAW IT AS HER DUTY TO FLY OUT HERE AND TAKE CARE OF DAD AND ME. SO SHE WORKED REALLY HARD THIS AFTERNOON TO MAKE SUPPER FOR THE THREE OF US. SHE MADE A VEGETABLE LASAGNA. IT WAS RUNNY, OVERCOOKED ON THE TOP, AND UNDERCOOKED IN THE MIDDLE. IT TOOK HER A LONG TIME TO MAKE IT. I AM TRYING TO BE APPRECIATIVE.

DAD AND AUNT MORGAN AND I ATE IN THE KITCHEN WITH THE DOOR INTO MOM'S ROOM OPEN SO SHE COULD HEAR US. I THINK MOM WAS ASLEEP THE WHOLE TIME, THOUGH. ALREADY I DON'T REMEMBER MUCH ABOUT DINNER. ONLY THAT I WASN'T HUNGRY, BUT THAT I FORCED SOME OF THE

LASAGNA DOWN. AND I TRIED TO ANSWER DAD'S
AND AUNT MORGAN'S QUESTIONS ABOUT SCHOOL AND
STUFF.

THEN I JUST LOOKED AT THE TWO OF THEM
SITTING THERE, ALL DEFEATED. AFTER A FEW
MOMENTS, I EXCUSED MYSELF.

WHY HAS EVERYONE GIVEN UP ON MOM?

I WANT TO YELL, "DON'T GIVE UP!
DON'T GIVE UP!" I EVEN WANT TO YELL THOSE
WORDS AT MOM. BECAUSE SHE HAS GIVEN UP TOO.
I KNOW SHE HAS. AND I DON'T UNDERSTAND WHY.

ALSO, I DON'T WANT THE END TO COME. I
AM NOT READY.

10:32 P.M.

I KNEW I WASN'T GOING TO DO ANY
HOMEWORK TONIGHT, BUT I DIDN'T EXPECT TO BE
SO BUSY. THE LAST FEW EVENINGS HAVE BEEN
QUIET, AND SOME OF MY SADDEST TIMES. THAT'S
WHY I KNEW I WOULDN'T BE ABLE TO
CONCENTRATE ON WORK. I THOUGHT I WOULD JUST
SIT AND WRITE.

BUT A COUPLE OF HOURS AGO, THE PHONE

STARTED TO RING. AND SINCE DAD'S SPENDING ALL HIS TIME WITH MOM, AND AUNT MORGAN WAS BUSY WITH HER EVERLASTING LAUNDRY CHORES, I WAS PUT IN CHARGE OF THE PHONE. THE FIRST CALLER WAS MR. SCHAFER, JUST CHECKING UP ON THINGS. FUNNY, FOR SOME REASON WHEN I HEARD A GUY'S VOICE I THOUGHT DUCKY WAS CALLING. I WAS DISAPPOINTED FOR A MOMENT BUT GLAD TO HEAR FROM DAWN'S FATHER. HE AND CAROL, ESPECIALLY CAROL, HAVE BEEN SO WONDERFUL. MAYBE I'LL GO TALK TO CAROL TOMORROW. MR. SCHAFER ASKED ME IF I WANTED TO TALK TO HER ON THE PHONE TONIGHT, BUT I'D RATHER TALK IN PERSON.

AFTER MR. SCHAFER CALLED, GRETA CALLED. I DON'T KNOW WHY, BUT I HAVE A LITTLE TROUBLE TALKING TO THOSE PEOPLE FROM MOM'S CANCER SUPPORT GROUP. THEY'RE ALL VERY NICE AND EVERYTHING, BUT   I DON'T KNOW HOW TO FINISH THIS SENTENCE. WHAT IS MY PROBLEM WITH GRETA AND THE OTHERS? NOT SURE. MAYBE IT'S THAT SO FAR THEY'RE SURVIVING THEIR CANCERS. AND MOM IS NOT. I TALKED TO GRETA FOR A FEW MINUTES, AND THEN SOMEONE FROM THE BOOKSTORE CALLED WITH QUESTIONS FOR DAD. I GUESS HE'S NOT DISPENSABLE AFTER ALL. I KNEW

DAD DIDN'T WANT TO BE DISTURBED, SO I TRIED
TO ANSWER THE QUESTIONS MYSELF. IT EVEN
OCCURRED TO ME THAT THIS WOULD BE A GOOD
EXCUSE TO CALL DUCKY FINALLY. HE'S SPENT TIME
WORKING AT THE BOOKSTORE. MAYBE HE COULD
ANSWER THE QUESTIONS. BUT I JUST COULDN'T GET
UP THE NERVE TO CALL HIM. I WONDER HOW LONG
THAT WILL TAKE.

OKAY. I'LL TRY GOING TO BED. MAYBE
TONIGHT IS THE NIGHT I'LL BE ABLE TO SLEEP AT
LAST.

11:18 P.M.

NO LUCK. TOSSING AND TURNING.

11:41 P.M.

THE LIGHT FROM THE STREET LAMP IS DRIVING
ME CRAZY. I CAN'T BLOCK IT OUT.

11:53 P.M.

WHAT HAS HAPPENED TO MY PILLOW? IT FEELS LIKE SOMEONE FLATTENED IT WITH A SLEDGEHAMMER.

WEDNESDAY 3/17
12:08 A.M.

OH MY GOD. THIS IS AWFUL. MOM IS MAKING THE MOST HORRIBLE NOISES DOWNSTAIRS. I'VE NEVER HEARD ANYTHING LIKE THEM. THIS IS NEW. DAD IS DOWN THERE WITH HER, OF COURSE, BUT WHAT DO I DO? SHOULD I GO TO HER? WHAT DO THE NOISES MEAN? IS THIS THE END? OH GOD, I CAN'T STAND IT IF THIS IS REALLY THE END. RIGHT NOW. RIGHT NOW. I'M STILL NOT READY.

I FEEL LIKE PRAYING. I HAVEN'T PRAYED SINCE I WAS A LITTLE KID.

NOW I LAY ME DOWN TO SLEEP. I PRAY THE LORD MY SOUL TO KEEP. IF I SHOULD DIE BEFORE I

OH GOD. I NEVER PAID MUCH ATTENTION TO THAT PRAYER BEFORE. IT'S HORRIBLE.

12:11 A.M.

THE NOISES HAVE STOPPED. WHAT DOES THAT MEAN? I KNOW I SHOULD GO DOWNSTAIRS BUT I'M AFRAID TO. I'M REALLY NOT PREPARED FOR IT TO BE OVER.

PLEASE. JUST LET ME HAVE A FEW MORE DAYS. THAT'S ALL I ASK.

I'M GOING DOWNSTAIRS NOW.

12:28 A.M.

MOM IS ASLEEP. DAD SAID HE'D NEVER SEEN HER IN SO MUCH PAIN. THE MORPHINE HAD WORN OFF, THE NURSE HAD GIVEN HER SOME MORE, AND IT HADN'T REALLY HELPED, SO SHE'D GIVEN HER EVEN MORE. IT TAKES LONGER AND LONGER FOR IT TO WORK. THE NOISES MOM WAS MAKING BEFORE WERE LIKE HOWLING. LIKE AN ANIMAL HOWLING.

I WAS SO SCARED WHEN I TIPTOED DOWNSTAIRS. I REALLY THOUGHT I MIGHT GO INTO MOM'S ROOM AND DAD WOULD SAY, "SUNNY, I'M SORRY, MOM IS GONE."

MY HEART WAS POUNDING AND MY MOUTH HAD GONE DRY. I STOOD AT THE BOTTOM OF THE

STAIRS FOR A SECOND AND LISTENED. I COULD HEAR MOM MOANING BUT NOT HOWLING LIKE BEFORE. THE ROOM WAS LIT BY A NIGHT-LIGHT AND THAT STREET LAMP. I PEEKED INTO MOM'S ROOM. I COULD SEE HER HUNCHED UP IN THE BED, THE NURSE HOVERING, AND DAD SITTING WITH HER, STROKING HER HAND, HER HAIR, TALKING SOFTLY TO HER. I REMEMBER WHEN MOM USED TO DO THAT FOR ME WHEN I WAS SICK.

I DIDN'T KNOW IF I SHOULD SAY ANYTHING, BUT FINALLY I WHISPERED, "DAD?"

"IT'S OKAY, HONEY," HE SAID. "THE MORPHINE IS STARTING TO WORK AGAIN. SHE'S GOING TO SLEEP."

I NODDED. I WENT INTO THE KITCHEN FOR SOMETHING TO DRINK. THEN I SAT IN THE LIVING ROOM AND STARED OUT THE WINDOW FOR A BIT. AFTER A FEW MINUTES, DAD JOINED ME AND WE TALKED A LITTLE. BUT NOT ABOUT ANYTHING IMPORTANT. AND THEN I CAME BACK TO BED.

10:16 A.M.

WHAT A NIGHT LAST NIGHT. THIS MORNING I DECIDED NOT EVEN TO GO TO SCHOOL. FOR ONE

THING, I THINK THE END REALLY IS NEAR. I COULDN'T BEAR TO BE AT SCHOOL AND NOT WITH MOM WHEN IT FINALLY COMES. FOR ANOTHER THING, I DON'T THINK I'VE EVER, EVER, BEEN SO BONE-WEARY TIRED AS I AM THIS MORNING.

LAST NIGHT, AFTER I TRIED TO GO BACK TO BED, I DECIDED I NEEDED TO SEE THE MOON. I LOOKED OUT MY WINDOW BUT I COULDN'T FIND IT. THEN I WANTED TO SMELL THE NIGHT AIR. I RAISED MY WINDOW. AND ACROSS THE YARD I SAW DAWN'S WINDOW BEING RAISED TOO.

"SUNNY?" SHE CALLED SOFTLY. "ARE YOU OKAY? I HEARD YOUR WINDOW OPEN."

"I CAN'T SLEEP. I WANTED TO SEE THE MOON AND SMELL THE AIR."

"I CAN'T SLEEP EITHER."

"MEET ME OUTSIDE?"

"OKAY."

IT WAS JUST LIKE WHEN WE WERE KIDS, ON HOT SUMMER NIGHTS WHEN WE COULDN'T SLEEP. WHY DID WE ALWAYS MEET IN MY YARD, I WONDER?

THREE MINUTES LATER WE WERE SITTING TOGETHER ON AN OLD LAWN CHAIR.

"REMEMBER WHEN WE USED TO COME OUT HERE WHEN WE WERE LITTLE?" DAWN SAID.

"I WAS JUST THINKING ABOUT THAT."

"What did we talk about then?"

"Stuff that scared us."

"Like what?"

"Kid stuff. Bad dreams. Shadows."

"Our dreams back then were so silly. Remember the one I had about the foxes under my bed?"

I smiled. "Yeah. Why were the foxes so scary?"

"I don't know. But they were REALLY scary. And you had that dream about the bulldog. Remember?"

"Yeah. You'd think we hated animals," I said.

"Have you been asleep at all tonight?" asked Dawn.

"Nope. Not one wink. How about you?"

"I fell asleep for about an hour and then I woke up. I was just lying there when I heard you."

"Mom was making noises downstairs. She's in a lot of pain tonight."

Dawn winced. "I'm sorry."

We leaned against the back of the lawn chair. We could just barely squeeze into it, side by side.

"WE USED TO FIT BETTER," SAID DAWN.

"REMEMBER THE TIME WE WERE SITTING ON THIS WITH MAGGIE AND JILL AND IT COLLAPSED?"

DAWN LAUGHED. "THEN WE ADDED UP OUR WEIGHTS AND ALTOGETHER THEY ONLY TOTALED, LIKE, THE WEIGHT OF ONE REALLY LARGE ADULT, SO WE COULDN'T FIGURE OUT WHY THE CHAIR WOULDN'T HOLD US."

"LIKE, THE FOUR OF US WEREN'T USING IT AS A TRAMPOLINE."

WE SAT QUIETLY FOR A FEW MINUTES AND GAZED AT THE SKY. NOW I COULD SEE THE MOON. IT WAS THE THINNEST OF CRESCENTS. JUST A HAIR.

AFTER AWHILE DAWN SAID, "SUNNY, DO YOU REMEMBER THE TIME YOUR MOM GAVE US THE PENNIES —"

I DIDN'T WANT TO THINK ABOUT THAT. "NOT NOW," I SAID, CUTTING HER OFF. A LITTLE CHATTING WAS OKAY, BUT I DIDN'T WANT A BIG TALK ABOUT MOM.

FOR JUST A SECOND DAWN LOOKED WOUNDED, BUT THEN HER FACE CHANGED. "ALL RIGHT," SHE SAID.

I AM SO, SO GLAD THAT DAWN AND I ARE FRIENDS AGAIN. I HAVE MY BEST FRIEND BACK, THE

PERSON WHO ALWAYS UNDERSTANDS ME. I CAN'T BELIEVE THAT I ALMOST LOST HER.

ONLY YOUR BEST FRIEND COULD UNDERSTAND EVERYTHING YOU MEAN WHEN YOU SAY JUST TWO WORDS, LIKE "NOT NOW."

11:50 A.M.

HAVE BEEN LOOKING IN MY CLOSET. WHAT A MESS. I'LL HAVE TO STRAIGHTEN IT OUT ONE DAY. FIRST I NEED TO CLEAN IT OUT. I BET I HAVE STUFF IN THERE FROM SECOND GRADE.

12:22 P.M.

THE DOCTOR JUST LEFT. HE LOOKED PRETTY GRIM. NOW DAD AND AUNT MORGAN LOOK GRIM TOO. I DIDN'T HANG AROUND TO HEAR WHAT THE DOCTOR SAID.

I DON'T WANT TO KNOW.

AUNT MORGAN HAS FIXED LUNCH BUT NONE OF US CAN EAT IT. DAD DOESN'T WANT TO LEAVE MOM'S SIDE, AND ANYWAY, HE DOESN'T HAVE AN APPETITE. NEITHER DO AUNT MORGAN OR I. SO THIS BOWL OF POTATO SALAD IS SITTING ON THE KITCHEN COUNTER WITH THREE CLEAN PLATES BESIDE IT. AUNT MORGAN HAS BEEN HERE FOR THREE DAYS AND THIS IS THE FIRST TIME SHE HASN'T INSISTED ON A "FAMILY MEAL." WE ARE ALL SO TIRED AND DRAWN-LOOKING.

1:15 P.M.

THERE'S THE WEIRDEST TALK SHOW ON TV. I ALMOST NEVER WATCH TV DURING THE DAY SO I DON'T KNOW — MAYBE THE SHOW ISN'T SO WEIRD. BUT ANYWAY, IT'S ALL ABOUT WOMEN WHO USED TO BE MARRIED TO OTHER GUYS AND NOW THEY'RE MARRIED TO THE GUYS' BROTHERS. TRULY. WHEN A NEW FACE COMES ON THE SCREEN A CAPTION WILL APPEAR THAT READS SOMETHING LIKE CINDY — BROTHER-IN-LAW IS ALSO EX-HUSBAND. SOME OF THE BROTHERS SEEM TO GET ALONG

PRETTY WELL. OTHERS, OF COURSE, ARE FURIOUS AT EACH OTHER. ONE CAPTION READ JOSEPH — HAS RESTRAINING ORDER AGAINST BROTHER.

WHY ARE PEOPLE INTERESTED IN THIS SORT OF THING? I'M MYSTIFIED.

1:28 P.M.

ALL RIGHT. I'LL ADMIT IT. I'M ALSO BORED. WELL, MAYBE I'M NOT REALLY BORED. I THINK I'M AFRAID. THE PROGRAM IS OVER AND NOW I'M JUST SITTING UP HERE IN MY ROOM, AFRAID TO GO DOWNSTAIRS. NOTHING HAS CHANGED. DAD HASN'T GIVEN ME ANY NEWS. I THINK MOM HAS ANOTHER VISITOR. BUT FOR SOME REASON I'M NOW AFRAID.

I GUESS MOM ISN'T GOING TO BE WITH US MUCH LONGER.

1:32 P.M.

BY "MUCH LONGER" I MEAN I THINK SHE IS GOING TO DIE IN THE NEXT DAY OR TWO.

1:47 P.M.

GOD, MY HAIR IS A MESS. I REALLY NEED TO
GET IT CUT.

2:26 P.M.

SCHOOL IS ALMOST OVER. I WONDER WHAT I
MISSED TODAY.

BUT I DON'T CARE.

2:39 P.M.

I JUST REALIZED THAT I HAVEN'T <u>DONE</u>
ANYTHING TODAY. I'M HIDING OUT IN MY ROOM,
SITTING, STARING OUT THE WINDOW, PICKING UP THE
JOURNAL EVERY SO OFTEN. I'VE BARELY TALKED TO
MOM OR DAD OR AUNT MORGAN. I WONDER IF
ANYONE REMEMBERED TO PUT AWAY THE POTATO
SALAD. I BETTER GO DO THAT BEFORE THE
MAYONNAISE GOES BAD.

OH, DOORBELL

STOPPED WRITING EARLIER TO ANSWER THE DOORBELL, AND SUDDENLY I WASN'T BORED ANYMORE. DIDN'T GET BACK TO THE JOURNAL UNTIL JUST NOW.

I COULD HEAR THE DOORBELL RING — AND THEN RING A SECOND AND A THIRD TIME. WHY DIDN'T DAD OR AUNT MORGAN ANSWER IT? ALL OF A SUDDEN THAT PANICKY FEELING OVERWHELMED ME ONCE MORE. MAYBE MOM HAD . . . MAYBE THAT'S WHY NO ONE COULD ANSWER THE DOOR. AGAIN MY HEART STARTED RACING AND I COULD FEEL THE BLOOD PULSING IN MY HEAD. MY MOUTH GOT DRY.

NOW I LAY ME DOWN TO SLEEP. I PRAY THE LORD MY SOUL TO KEEP.

DING-DONG.

MY LEADEN FEET DRAGGED ME OUT OF MY ROOM AND DOWN THE STAIRS. AND I HEAVED A SIGH OF RELIEF. AUNT MORGAN WAS ON THE PHONE AND DAD WAS BUSY WITH MOM. I BET HE HADN'T EVEN HEARD THE BELL.

I WAS SHAKING WHEN I ANSWERED THE DOOR.

"HI, SUNNY."

MOM'S FRIEND ANNE WAS ON OUR FRONT

STOOP. SHE LOOKED TIRED AND DRAWN LIKE THE REST OF US. I TRIED TO REMEMBER IF SHE'D BEEN HERE YESTERDAY. I THINK SHE MIGHT HAVE BEEN. AND THE DAY BEFORE. SHE CAME TO THE HOSPITAL NEARLY EVERY DAY TOO.

"HI," I REPLIED.

"HOW IS SHE TODAY?"

"THE SAME. NO, MAYBE A LITTLE WORSE. COME ON IN." I KNOW ANNE IS ALWAYS WELCOME. MOM HAS WANTED TO SEE HER NO MATTER WHAT.

I WALKED WITH ANNE TO MOM'S ROOM AND LEFT HER THERE. SHE GREETED DAD, BUT THEN TO MY SURPRISE, DAD LEFT THE ROOM AND SAT IN THE KITCHEN, GIVING MOM AND ANNE TIME ALONE TOGETHER, I GUESS. I THOUGHT DAD'S EYES LOOKED A LITTLE RED. WELL, OF COURSE. HE WAS OPERATING ON ALMOST NO SLEEP.

WHEN ANNE LEFT MOM'S ROOM ABOUT TWENTY MINUTES LATER, HER EYES WERE RED TOO. ACTUALLY, SHE WAS CRYING. ACTUALLY, SHE WAS SOBBING. I WONDERED IF SHE HAD BEEN SOBBING WITH MOM, OR IF MOM HAD BEEN ASLEEP, OR IF ANNE HAD JUST NOW BEGUN TO CRY. I FELT AS IF I WERE WATCHING THE SCENE FROM VERY, VERY FAR AWAY.

Anne came over to me again, cupped my chin in her hand, and looked into my eyes for a moment before leaving the house.

I didn't say anything.

Ten minutes later, the doorbell rang again and this time Grandma and Grandad were there.

"Hi!" I greeted them. Suddenly I felt all perky.

Grandma gave me an odd look, though. "Hi, honey," she said softly.

"I guess you want to see Mom."

"Well, yes."

No one said so, but suddenly I had the feeling that Grandma and Grandad were here to say good-bye to Mom. I squashed the feeling. I led them to Mom's room, then rushed outside and sat on the stoop.

That was how I happened to see Dawn come home from school. Ducky drove her in his old wreck of a car. He pulled into Dawn's driveway and turned off the ignition. The two of them started to walk into the Schafers' house. Then Dawn spotted me. She waved. "Hi, Sunny," she called, but she wasn't smiling.

"Hi," I replied.

Dawn headed across the lawn toward me, but behind her, Ducky hesitated. Dawn turned to him. "Come on," she said.

"No, I better —"

"Come on."

This was horrible. Ducky was afraid of me, I think. And I couldn't blame him. What I did to him was terrible.

I jumped up. "Ducky?" I called.

"Yeah?"

"Can we talk?"

8:01 P.M.

Had to stop for dinner, which was horrible. Not the food. Just the whole thing. Dad and Aunt Morgan and I sat at the kitchen table and picked at the potato salad and didn't say much. We still weren't hungry, but I guess we thought we shouldn't skip two meals in a row.

I have lost seven pounds.

Now I am back upstairs, safe in my room.

* * *

Anyway, Ducky finally followed Dawn across the lawn. He looked almost frantic when Dawn said, "Sunny, can I go see your mother?"

I knew he didn't want to be left alone with me. I also knew that Dawn was purposely leaving him alone with me. Not to be mean, but because we needed to talk.

Ducky and I sat on the front porch.

"Ducky —" I began. And then all the dreadful things I said and did to him the night of the concert came flooding back to me. How could I have said those things? Done those things? It was like some other person was saying and doing them. Not me. "Ducky," I said again. "Um —"

"Sunny," Ducky said at the same time, "I —"

"No, let me go first."

"Okay." Once again, Ducky looked almost afraid of me.

I barged ahead. "Ducky, I want to apologize. You're one of my best friends. I don't know why I said those things. I didn't mean them. I just wanted to hurt you."

Ducky's expression changed from wary to angry. "If I'm such a good friend, why did you want to hurt me? Is that how you treat all your good friends?"

"No, of course not."

"Just the ones you think you can step on?"

"Ducky, please," I said. I was surprised but almost glad to hear that he was so mad. "I thought if I could embarrass you, then you would drive us home after all. I didn't want to go home in disgrace with Mr. Schafer. I wanted a perfect, grown-up evening. I had this fantasy about the evening. It had been keeping my mind off Mom. And I didn't want anything to spoil it."

Ducky softened a little, but all he said was, "Then why did you keep giving me drinks?"

"I don't know. The drinks were part of the perfect, grown-up evening. I just wasn't thinking ahead to what would happen when it was time for you to drive. But Ducky, I'm really, really, really sorry. You truly are one of my best friends. I know I hurt you, but I hope we can be friends again. I've missed you."

Now Ducky softened completely. "I'm sorry too."

"What are you sorry about?"

"I'm sorry I haven't been here for you."

I shrugged. I'm sorry about that too, but it was my own fault.

"Sunny?" said Ducky when I didn't say anything. "Speak to me."

I smiled. Ducky is one of the few people who can make me smile these days. "Speak to you about what?" I said, even though I knew perfectly well what he meant.

"Tell me exactly what is going on with your mom right now. I know what Dawn tells me, but I want to hear it from you. Also, how you're feeling, what you're thinking. You know."

Here's the thing about Ducky. If almost anyone else said that to me (tell me what you're thinking or tell me what you're feeling) I would reply with something rude and sarcastic like, "My mother is dying. How do you think I feel?" Or, "My mother is dying. That's what I'm thinking about." But I knew Ducky really wanted to know specifically what

WAS GOING ON WITH MOM. AND SPECIFICALLY WHAT MY INNERMOST THOUGHTS ARE. (DUCKY IS ALMOST LIKE THIS JOURNAL.) SO IF I WAS THINKING, "THIS IS SO HARD AND PAINFUL THAT I WISH MOM WOULD JUST DIE NOW AND GET IT OVER WITH," THAT IS WHAT I COULD SAY TO DUCKY, AND HE WOULDN'T THINK I WAS A HORRIBLE PERSON.

I DREW IN A BREATH. "WELL," I BEGAN, "THE DOCTOR WAS HERE A COUPLE OF HOURS AGO."

"DID YOU TALK TO HIM?" DUCKY INTERRUPTED ME.

"NO. I DIDN'T EVEN GO DOWNSTAIRS. I KIND OF DIDN'T WANT TO KNOW WHAT'S GOING ON."

DUCKY NODDED. "I UNDERSTAND."

"BUT AFTER HE LEFT?" (DUCKY NODDED AGAIN.) "DAD AND AUNT MORGAN LOOKED KIND OF, I DON'T KNOW, STUNNED MAYBE."

DUCKY SUCKED AIR BETWEEN HIS TEETH. "WHOA."

"YEAH. I KNOW. AND THEN PEOPLE STARTED COMING OVER. WELL, NOT A WHOLE STREAM OF THEM, BUT FIRST ANNE SHOWED UP" (DUCKY HAS MET ANNE ONCE OR TWICE), "AND NOW GRANDMA AND GRANDAD ARE HERE. WHEN ANNE WAS HERE DAD LEFT MOM'S ROOM TO LET HER SEE MOM alone. And Anne gave me this really long look when she left. Like, a long meaningful look?"

"Yeah?"

"And she was crying really hard, and she didn't even try to say anything to me."

"Whoa."

"Grandma and Grandad are very serious," I went on. "I was happy to see them, but Grandma looked at me kind of strangely. Like, how could I even think of seeming happy right now." I paused. "Hey. I wonder what Dawn's doing, because when she went inside Grandma and Grandad were still with Mom, I think. Hold on a second," I said to Ducky.

I stuck my head in the front door. I saw that the door to the dining room was ajar and I could hear low voices from inside. Then I peered into the living room. There were Dad and Dawn, sitting on the couch, not talking, just sitting. So Dawn probably hadn't seen Mom yet.

"Ducky," I said when I joined him on the porch again. "Ducky, I just want to say this one more time. You mean so much to me. I'm so sorry I was such a bad friend to someone who's been such a good friend." I almost added, "I love you," because I do, but something stopped me.

Ducky looked at me then with huge eyes that were soon filled with tears. He couldn't say a word. He just turned to me and gave me a hug. That was when I knew that everything would be okay between us.

Ducky and I sat quietly on the porch for awhile. Just sat. Side by side. Every now and then, Ducky took my hand. After fifteen minutes or so had gone by I stuck my head in the front door again. Now Dad and Aunt Morgan were sitting in the living room with Grandma and Grandad, and Dawn had disappeared.

"Dawn's with Mom," I reported to Ducky.

A few more minutes went by and Ducky and I heard the front door open. We turned around and saw Grandma and Grandad.

"Call us," Grandma was saying to Dad.

"No matter what time, son," Grandad added, and touched Dad's shoulder. I have always thought that Dad is lucky to have parents like Grandma and Grandad.

Dad closed the front door, and Ducky and I stood up.

"You remember Ducky?" I said.

Ducky stuck out his hand and first Grandma, then Grandad shook it. But nobody said anything.

Then Grandma turned to me. "You too, honey," she said. "You call us anytime. For any reason."

"Okay," I replied. I wasn't sure why she said that because I thought it was kind of understood. I mean, I call them plenty of times for plenty of reasons.

Grandad hugged me then and stepped off the porch. Grandma took my hand and held it and looked deep into my eyes. She started to say something, then pursed her lips to keep from crying, turned, and followed Grandad. They got into their car and pulled out of the driveway.

Ducky and I looked at each other. Finally I said, "Want to go inside?"

Ducky looked like that was the very last thing he wanted to do, but he said, "Sure," stood up, and held the door open for me.

Dad and Aunt Morgan were standing in the kitchen, conferring about something. The

DOOR TO MOM'S ROOM WAS STILL AJAR. IT OPENED
SLOWLY AND DAWN TIPTOED OUT. SHE WAS CRYING.

"WHAT —" I STARTED TO SAY.

BUT DAWN HELD HER FINGER TO HER LIPS.
"SHH," SHE SAID VERY, VERY QUIETLY. AND SHE
HEADED FOR THE FRONT DOOR. SO DUCKY AND I
TURNED AROUND AND FOLLOWED HER BACK OUTSIDE.

DUCKY LOOKED AT DAWN'S TEARSTAINED FACE
AND HELD HIS ARMS OUT TO HER. HE ENVELOPED
HER IN A BEAR HUG. AND ONCE AGAIN A COLD
FEAR WASHED OVER ME. HAD MOM . . . ? NO, SHE
COULDN'T HAVE. DAD AND AUNT MORGAN WOULDN'T
HAVE BEEN TALKING SO CALMLY IN THE KITCHEN.
THEY WOULD HAVE BEEN IN MOM'S ROOM. OR ON
THE PHONE OR SOMETHING.

I WAITED UNTIL THE FEAR HAD MELTED AWAY,
SIGHED HUGELY, AND THEN SAID, "DAWN, WHAT IS
IT?"

DUCKY RELEASED DAWN FROM THE HUG AND SHE
TURNED TO ME. SHE WAS STILL TOO CHOKED UP TO
SPEAK, BUT I HAD THE FEELING THAT EVEN IF
SHE COULD HAVE SPOKEN, SHE WOULDN'T HAVE
WANTED TO.

"SUNNY," SAID DUCKY, "I'M GOING TO WALK
DAWN HOME."

"OKAY. I'M GLAD YOU GUYS CAME OVER."

"ME TOO," REPLIED DUCKY. "WANT ME TO
CALL YOU TONIGHT?"

"SURE. DEFINITELY."

DAWN AND DUCKY LEFT AND I WENT INTO
THE HOUSE AGAIN. I HADN'T SPOKEN TO MOM IN
HOURS AND I KNEW I HAD TO GO INTO HER
ROOM.

SO I DID.

                                                    9:58 P.M.

QUIET. NOTHING GOING ON DOWNSTAIRS. THE
PHONE HAS RUNG A COUPLE OF TIMES. THAT'S ALL.

DAD AND AUNT MORGAN WERE STILL IN THE
KITCHEN. THEY WERE SITTING AT THE TABLE WITH
SOME PAPERS SPREAD AROUND THEM. I SIGNALED
THAT I WAS GOING IN TO SEE MOM AND THEY
NODDED.

I STEPPED INTO MOM'S ROOM, WHICH WE'VE
BEEN KEEPING DARK. FOR SOME REASON, THE LIGHT
SOMETIMES HURTS MOM'S EYES. SHE WAS LYING ON
HER BED, LOOKING PALER THAN EVER. HONESTLY,
HER SKIN SOMETIMES LOOKS TRANSLUCENT. YOU CAN

SEE HER VEINS IN PLACES — PLACES YOU WOULDN'T
EXPECT TO BE ABLE TO SEE THEM. HER BREATHING
WAS SHALLOW AND HER EYES WERE HALF OPEN.

"MOM?" I WHISPERED.

HER EYES OPENED. "HI, HONEY. HOW WAS
SCHOOL?"

I DIDN'T HAVE THE HEART TO TELL HER THAT
THE REASON I HADN'T VISITED HER ALL DAY WAS
NOT BECAUSE I'D BEEN AT SCHOOL, BUT BECAUSE I
WAS A GREAT BIG COWARD.

"WELL . . ." I BEGAN. WAS I ACTUALLY
GOING TO LIE TO MY MOTHER? LIE TO HER NOW?
I COULDN'T DO THAT. BUT THEN, I REALLY
COULDN'T TELL HER I'D BEEN HOME THE ENTIRE DAY
AND HADN'T COME INTO HER ROOM EVEN ONCE.
FINALLY I SAID, "IT WAS ABOUT THE SAME." I
FIGURED THAT PROBABLY WASN'T A LIE. I WAS SURE
SCHOOL HAD BEEN ABOUT THE SAME. I JUST HADN'T
BEEN THERE.

OKAY, OKAY. I FEEL VERY BAD ABOUT HAVING
SAID THAT, BUT IT'S OVER AND DONE. I CAN'T
TAKE IT BACK.

"TELL ME WHAT'S GOING ON," SAID MOM.

I LOOKED AT HER CLOSELY. I THOUGHT SHE
SEEMED A BIT MORE ALERT THAN USUAL. HER EYES
HAD OPENED AND HER VOICE SEEMED STRONGER.

"What's going on?"

"Yes," said Mom. "In your life. How are you and Dawn getting along these days? How is Ducky? What are you working on in school?"

I settled in on Mom's bed for a talk. We hadn't had one in awhile. This was nice.

"Dawn and I are friends again. But I guess you knew that. I mean, from talking to Dawn. It's like before anything happened. Like old times."

"That's nice," said Mom.

"Mm-hm. And Ducky is good. He was here a few minutes ago, but he didn't come in."

"That's okay."

"Mom, I didn't tell you that Ducky and I had a fight. A big one. But we made up. Just now. And I'm really glad."

"What was the fight about?"

"Oh, it's a long story."

I didn't feel like telling Mom the story. Not because she wouldn't understand, but just because I wanted to talk about other things. It was so nice to be sitting here sharing stuff with her. We hadn't done that in a long, long time. She hadn't felt well enough.

Did she actually feel better now? I had to know.

"Mom? You look a little better today."

Mom smiled apologetically. "Well, that's nice, honey. Thank you for saying so."

"But — ?"

"But . . . I'm in a lot of pain." I must have looked confused because she said, "The doctor gave me a new pain medication and right after I take it I feel great for a little while."

"Oh."

Disappointment.

10:48 P.M.

Continuing after a phone call from Ducky . . .

I have seen Mom in all sorts of states over the past year or so. I have seen her bald. I have seen her barfing from the chemo. I have seen her so tired that reaching for a glass wears her out. I have seen her so lifeless I thought she had died. I look at

THIS NEWEST MOM. SHE SEEMS A LITTLE BETTER, AND NOW I LEARN THAT'S BECAUSE SHE'S ACTUALLY WORSE. SHE'S IN SO MUCH PAIN THAT SHE'S ON SUPER-STRENGTH MEDICATION THAT MAKES HER FEEL BETTER FOR A WHILE, THEN DROPS HER BACK INTO SOME ABYSS OF MISERY I CAN'T COMPREHEND OR IMAGINE.

I DECIDED TO TAKE ADVANTAGE OF MOM'S DRUG-INDUCED CONDITION TO HAVE A REAL TALK WITH HER, THOUGH.

"MOM," I SAID, "TELL ME ABOUT WHEN I WAS A BABY." I SWEAR, I DO NOT KNOW WHERE THAT CAME FROM. IT SOUNDS LIKE SOMETHING AN EIGHT-YEAR-OLD WOULD SAY. BUT THE WORDS FELL OUT OF MY MOUTH.

I THINK MOM WAS AS STARTLED BY THEM AS I WAS. "WHAT?" SHE SAID.

"WHEN I WAS A BABY, YOUR BABY, WHAT WAS I LIKE?"

"WELL . . ." MOM SEARCHED FOR WORDS. "YOU WERE SUNNY. YOUR PERSONALITY, I MEAN, I THINK WE WOULD HAVE NICKNAMED YOU SUNNY EVEN IF YOUR NAME WASN'T SUNSHINE. YOU SMILED ALL THE TIME, AND EVERYTHING MADE YOU LAUGH, EVEN THINGS THAT MIGHT HAVE FRIGHTENED OTHER BABIES."

"LIKE WHAT?"

"LIKE THUNDER OR A BIG DOG OR BEING TAKEN TO A STRANGE PLACE. SOME BABIES WOULD HAVE CRIED. BUT YOU WOULD LOOK AT US AND LAUGH. WE WERE DELIGHTED. MOSTLY BECAUSE YOU WERE SO DELIGHTED."

(GOD. I'M LOOKING AT MYSELF IN THE MIRROR RIGHT NOW AND I DO NOT SEE A DELIGHTFUL, SUNNY PERSON. I SEE SOMEONE DRESSED IN BLACK JEANS AND NASTY-LOOKING BLACK BOOTS, A BLACK T-SHIRT, AND BLACK JEWELRY. MY HAIR IS DIRTY, AND I HARDLY EVER SMILE ANYMORE.)

"YOU WERE A GREAT BABY," MOM WENT ON. "THE BEST. IDEAL. LIKE A BABY OUT OF A FAIRY TALE. YOUR DAD AND I WERE IN LOVE WITH EACH OTHER AND IN LOVE WITH YOU. SOMETIMES WE WOULD SAY, 'HOW CAN TWO PEOPLE BE SO LUCKY? WE LEAD CHARMED LIVES.'"

I MARVELED THAT MOM COULD SAY THIS. DOES SHE STILL THINK SHE HAS LED A CHARMED LIFE?

"HOW COME YOU AND DAD NEVER HAD ANY OTHER KIDS?" I ASKED.

MOM DIDN'T ANSWER RIGHT AWAY. "WE WEREN'T ABLE TO," SHE SAID AT LAST. "WE WANTED OTHER CHILDREN, BECAUSE WE LIKED YOU SO MUCH. WE THOUGHT, 'IF ALL BABIES ARE AS WONDERFUL AS sunny, then we want lots of them.' But it wasn't meant to be. And we were already very happy with what we had. The three of us seemed like the perfect family."

But the problem with three, I thought, is that it's such a small number. When one of the three goes, only two are left. And when one of THEM goes, well, you're alone.

I tried to bring on a smile for Mom, though. "Okay, so I was a great baby. What was I like as a little girl?"

"Still pretty sunny. And adventurous. Do you remember the time you visited Mrs. Myrick?"

"Mrs. Myrick? When we lived in Grove Park?"

"Yes."

"Didn't we visit her a lot?"

"We did. But I'm thinking of a time you visited her alone. When you were three. This was how we met Mrs. Myrick in the first place."

"I guess I don't remember," I said.

"It was a Saturday morning. You and Dad and I were in the yard. Dad and I were working in the garden, and you were playing with your dump truck."

"I had a dump truck?"

"It was your favorite toy for several months." (I laughed.) "Anyway, I was pulling weeds, and suddenly I realized you were gone. Dad and I looked in the yard first, of course. Then we searched the house. Then we went back outside and began calling and calling for you. I asked Dad if I should phone the police and he said yes, so I did that, and while we waited for them to arrive we walked up and down the street, calling some more. A few of the neighbors joined us. We were several blocks away from our house when we heard you call out, 'Hi, Mommy! Hi, Daddy!' You were sitting on Mrs. Myrick's front porch, and the two of you were having a pretend tea party. You had just wandered there by yourself. Mrs. Myrick didn't know you, but she didn't think you should be off on your own yet, and she was trying to figure out who you were so she could call your parents. Of course, just at that moment the police showed up, and Dad and I were

EMBARRASSED BUT SO GLAD TO HAVE YOU BACK SAFE AND SOUND THAT WE DIDN'T CARE TOO MUCH. AFTER THAT, MRS. MYRICK BECAME ONE OF OUR BEST FRIENDS."

"I CAN'T BELIEVE I DID THAT!" I SAID. "HEY, MOM. TELL ME ABOUT YOU WHEN YOU WERE LITTLE. WERE YOU LIKE ME?"

"OH, NO, I WAS NOTHING LIKE YOU," SAID MOM. "TOTALLY DIFFERENT. SCARED OF EVERYTHING." MOM PAUSED AND HAD TO CATCH HER BREATH.

"YOU WERE SCARED OF EVERYTHING? BUT YOU'RE SO BRAVE," I SAID.

"ME? I'M NOT BRAVE!"

"YES, YOU ARE. LOOK AT WHAT YOU'VE BEEN THROUGH THIS YEAR. I WOULDN'T HAVE BEEN HALF AS BRAVE."

MOM SMILED RUEFULLY. "I DIDN'T EXACTLY HAVE A CHOICE."

"I STILL THINK YOU'RE BRAVE," I SAID.

"WELL . . . THANK YOU." SHE CLOSED HER EYES BRIEFLY.

"TELL ME SOMETHING NAUGHTY YOU DID WHEN YOU WERE LITTLE."

"HMM, NAUGHTY," SAID MOM, HER EYES STILL

CLOSED. "LET ME THINK. DID I EVER TELL YOU ABOUT THE TIME WITH THE CHICKENS?"

I LAUGHED. "NO."

"I WAS IN FIRST GRADE. AND OUR TEACHER —"

"WHAT WAS HER NAME? OR HIS NAME?" I INTERRUPTED.

"HER NAME. MRS. RAGO. AND MRS. RAGO BROUGHT A CAGE OF CHICKENS TO OUR ROOM ONE DAY. JUST FOR FUN. I DECIDED I WANTED TO SEE THEM OUT OF THE CAGE, NOT STUCK IN IT. SO I LET THEM OUT. THEY RAN AND FLAPPED AROUND THE ROOM, AND MRS. RAGO MADE ME STAND IN THE CORNER."

"OH, MOM! MRS. RAGO SOUNDS MEAN," I SAID. "BUT IT'S A FUNNY STORY."

"YOU KNOW WHAT I THINK IS FUNNY? THAT WAS ONE OF THE BRAVEST THINGS I DID AS A CHILD — AND IT INVOLVED CHICKENS. GET IT? CHICKENS?"

"I GET IT." I WAS LAUGHING AGAIN, EVEN THOUGH MOM WAS WHEEZING AND LAUGHING. THIS WAS SO NICE. MOM AND ME. JUST HANGING OUT, TALKING. "I'M GOING TO WRITE THAT DOWN," I TOLD MOM. "I REALLY LIKE THAT STORY. IT'S A

FUN WAY TO —" MY SENTENCE CAME TO A
SCREECHING HALT. I HAD ALMOST SAID "A FUN WAY
TO REMEMBER YOU." "I MEAN," I CONTINUED, "IT'S
A FUN MEMORY."

MOM DIDN'T ANSWER ME. SHE STARTED TO
COUGH THEN, AND IT MADE HER DOUBLE OVER.

"IS THE PAIN MEDICINE WEARING OFF?" I
ASKED ANXIOUSLY.

"I'M AFRAID SO." MOM WAS CLUTCHING HER CHEST.

I PEEKED THROUGH MOM'S DOOR AND SAW TO
MY RELIEF THAT THE NURSE WAS WAITING. I
SIGNALED TO HER. THE NURSE HURRIED INTO THE
ROOM AND FUSSED OVER MOM FOR A FEW MINUTES.

"WHY DON'T YOU REST NOW, MRS. WINSLOW?"
SHE SAID, AND MOM NODDED WEAKLY.

I HOPE I HAVE GOTTEN EVERYTHING DOWN,
EVERYTHING WE SAID THIS AFTERNOON. I DON'T
WANT TO FORGET ONE WORD OF IT.

THURSDAY 3/18
3:22 A.M.

WHOA. I JUST WOKE UP FROM THE MOST
HORRIBLE DREAM. I WAS IN MY BEDROOM AND

SOMEHOW I KNEW THAT A MAN WAS TRYING TO GET INTO MY ROOM. HE WAS ON THE OTHER SIDE OF MY DOOR, HOLDING A HUGE QUILT, AND HE PLANNED TO SMOTHER ME WITH THE QUILT. I COULD HEAR HIM RATTLING THE DOOR HANDLE.

I WOKE UP SWEATING.

THE FIRST TIME IN WEEKS THAT I'VE ACTUALLY BEEN IN A DEEP SLEEP.

WHEN I FIRST WOKE UP I THOUGHT I HEARD MOM DOWNSTAIRS, THOUGHT I HEARD HER MOANING, BUT WHEN I LISTENED AT MY DOOR (WHICH I WAS TERRIFIED OF OPENING BECAUSE OF THAT MAN WITH THE QUILT) I HEARD NOTHING.

5:46 A.M.

I WAS ABLE TO GO BACK TO SLEEP FOR A COUPLE OF HOURS, AND NOW I'M UP AGAIN. I GRABBED FOR THE JOURNAL RIGHT AWAY. I WANT TO RECORD EVERYTHING. EVERYTHING I CAN ABOUT THESE DAYS.

THESE LAST FEW DAYS.

SOMETHING HAPPENED AT DINNER LAST NIGHT, AFTER I'D TALKED TO MOM.

DAD AND I WERE ALONE IN THE KITCHEN. AUNT MORGAN WAS WITH MOM, EVEN THOUGH MOM WAS ASLEEP, AND EVEN THOUGH THE NURSE WAS HERE. DAD AND I WERE SUPPOSEDLY EATING DINNER, ALTHOUGH ONCE AGAIN WE WERE JUST SITTING IN FRONT OF PLATES OF UNTOUCHED FOOD. AND WE WERE BARELY SPEAKING.

AFTER A LONG, LONG PAUSE, DAD SAID, "SUNNY, YOU DON'T HAVE TO GO TO SCHOOL ANYMORE. I MEAN, UNTIL AFTER . . . YOU KNOW . . ."

(NOBODY WANTS TO SAY ANYTHING TOO CASUAL ABOUT MOM'S DYING. WE TALK ABOUT IT AND WE DON'T TALK ABOUT IT.)

"YOU'RE GIVING ME PERMISSION NOT TO GO TO SCHOOL?"

"WELL, IT'LL ONLY BE FOR A COUPLE OF —" DAD STOPPED HIMSELF.

OF COURSE I HAD FIGURED THIS OUT FOR MYSELF. ALL OF IT. THAT MOM HAD ONLY A DAY OR SO LEFT, AND THAT I COULD STAY HOME UNTIL SHE DIED. AFTER ALL, I'M ALREADY STAYING HOME. (HAS DAD NOTICED?) BUT WHEN I HEARD DAD SAY THESE WORDS, THAT COLD FEAR CAME OVER ME AGAIN. IT WAS AS IF AS LONG AS THOSE THOUGHTS STAYED INSIDE MY HEAD, MAYBE I HAD MADE THEM up. But now Dad was saying them, so they must be true.

"What do you mean?" I said to Dad.

"I think you know," he replied.

"Yeah. I know that you've given up on Mom. You and everyone else. You have all given up."

"Sunny —"

"Well, it's true. I just don't understand why. Why have you all given up?"

"Sunny —"

"No one talks about the future. No one even talks about next week. It's like there is no future."

"Sunny," said Dad flatly. "I thought you understood. Mom's treatments have been stopped and nothing more can be done for her. We have talked about all of this."

"I know." I stared down at my plate. "But how could this happen? How could we let it happen? It's like we're killing Mom."

I though Dad might get angry at that, but instead he said, "It does feel that way. You just have to remember that the way things feel isn't always the way things are. Mom's treatments were more painful than

HELPFUL. AND WHEN SHE DIES HER MISERY WILL FINALLY BE OVER."

"I KNOW," I WHISPERED. "I JUST DON'T REALLY UNDERSTAND ANY OF IT."

"NEITHER DO I," SAID DAD.

"THE NEW PAIN STUFF IS HELPING HER, THOUGH, ISN'T IT?"

"A LITTLE, YES. IT BUYS HER TIME. AND THERE ARE SOME THINGS SHE WANTS TO DO."

MY HEART LEAPED. "YOU MEAN LIKE PLACES SHE WANTS TO VISIT?"

"OH, HONEY, NO," SAID DAD QUICKLY. "THE PAIN MEDICATION DOES NOTHING MORE THAN WHAT YOU SAW IT DO THIS AFTERNOON. TAKE AWAY HER PAIN LONG ENOUGH FOR HER TO HAVE CONVERSATIONS OR VISITS WITH PEOPLE, OR TO WRITE A BIT. THERE ARE A FEW THINGS SHE WANTS TO PUT IN ORDER BEFORE SHE DIES."

"LIKE WHAT?"

"I'M NOT ENTIRELY SURE. SHE HAS SHARED SOME THINGS WITH ME, AND SHE'S CHOSEN TO KEEP OTHERS PRIVATE FOR NOW."

"IS SHE SAYING GOOD-BYE TO PEOPLE?" I ASKED, EVEN THOUGH I KNEW THE ANSWER.

"YES."

"Did she say good-bye to Anne this afternoon?"

"Yes."

"And to Grandma and Grandad?"

"Yes."

I nodded. "I thought so." And somehow I knew, I just knew, that she had NOT said good-bye to Dawn, even though Dawn had been awfully upset when she left Mom.

"You know, we should be preparing our own good-byes," said Dad.

"No."

"I don't like to think about it either, but I know Mom is preparing her good-byes to us."

My eyes filled with tears. "No," I said again.

Dad sighed. "Sunny, I wish I could say to you, 'Okay, we'll think about it another time,' but the truth is that we really don't have very much time."

"How much do we have?"

"A day or two, probably. Maybe three."

Three days is actually more time than I thought we had.

"This is undoubtedly the hardest thing you will ever have to do, Sunny," said Dad.

I waited for him to say, "But I know it will be fine." He didn't, though. He just looked at me.

"How do we prepare our good-byes?" I asked him.

Dad was silent for several moments. "Well, I don't know exactly," he said finally. "I guess we think about the things we don't want left unsaid."

The things we don't want left unsaid. What are those? What on earth are those? Mom knows I love her, but I guess I should say so, tell her. What else?

This is what I'm thinking now, but not what I thought as I sat across the table from Dad. I just felt numb then. I don't think I thought anything. My mind couldn't even wrap itself around any words. I stared at Dad. Then I stood up and ran out of the kitchen.

I know Dad thought I was mad at him, but I wasn't. I was consumed by that numbness and didn't know what to do. I

DIDN'T EVEN KNOW WHERE TO GO WHEN I LEFT THE
KITCHEN. I STEPPED INTO THE LIVING ROOM, THEN
BACK OUT, THEN INTO THE BATHROOM, FEELING SICK,
THEN BACK OUT, WENT TO MY ROOM, GOT OUT THE
JOURNAL, PUT IT BACK. FINALLY I RETURNED TO
THE KITCHEN.

DAD WAS SITTING AT THE TABLE, IN EXACTLY
THE SAME POSITION IN WHICH I'D LEFT HIM.

"YOU'RE RIGHT," I SAID.

6:38 A.M.

MOM IS AWAKE DOWNSTAIRS. I CAN HEAR DAD
AND AUNT MORGAN MOVING AROUND, DOING
MORNING THINGS. I CAN SMELL COFFEE BREWING,
THE CHINK OF DISHES. ANOTHER DAY IS STARTING.
THIS SOUNDS SO MELODRAMATIC, BUT I HAVE TO
ASK, IS THIS MOM'S LAST DAY? I WONDER: IF I
KNEW A PARTICULAR DAY WERE GOING TO BE MY
LAST DAY, HOW WOULD I WANT THAT DAY TO GO?
WHAT WOULD I WANT TO DO, SEE, EAT, FEEL,
HEAR, REMEMBER? MOM DOESN'T HAVE A LOT OF
CHOICES, BUT WE COULD STILL TRY TO MAKE HER
LAST DAYS AS SPECIAL AS POSSIBLE.

* * *

Last night when I returned to the kitchen I walked around behind Dad's chair and gave him an awkward hug. Then I said, "I think I'll sit with Mom now for awhile."

"Maybe I'll join you," said Dad.

Dad and Aunt Morgan and I have been trying to sit with Mom one at a time so as not to overwhelm her, but when Dad and I both entered Mom's room Aunt Morgan just moved over and made room for me on the bed. Dad sat in the armchair next to the bed.

"How nice," whispered Mom. "You're all here."

"The nurse gave your mom an injection," Aunt Morgan said to me. "She should be feeling better in a few minutes."

Sure enough, Mom began to rally, and twenty minutes later the four of us were chatting away.

"Morgan," said Mom, "tell Sunny what you felt would be an appropriate baby gift when she was born."

Aunt Morgan and Dad began to laugh. "Oh, no! That was deranged!" cried Aunt Morgan.

"Tell me," I said. I couldn't imagine what they were laughing about.

"No!" said Aunt Morgan.

"Okay, then I'll tell," said Mom. "Sunny, two days after you were born, your Aunt Morgan flew out here and showed up at our house bearing a huge bottle of vodka. A pink ribbon was tied around its neck."

I wrinkled my nose. "Vodka for a BABY?" I said.

"No, for your parents!" exclaimed Aunt Morgan. "I couldn't think of a better gift for two adults who were about to have their entire lives turned upside down."

At first I was speechless. Was that all a baby meant to Aunt Morgan? But then I began to laugh too. My stiff aunt Morgan had done THAT? I couldn't believe it. It put her in a whole new light.

"Of course, half an hour later," Mom went on in her raspy voice, "Morgan disappeared into the spare bedroom and emerged with a shopping bag full of the most wonderful presents for you. Italian baby clothes, a collection of picture books, and Baba."

"Baba? Baba came from Aunt Morgan? I didn't know that," I said.

What a fascinating piece of information. My beloved blanket had been a gift from Aunt Morgan. She was becoming more interesting by the moment.

"Hey, Aunt Morgan," I said. "This afternoon Mom told me about the time she let the chickens loose in her first-grade classroom. Tell me about something naughty that you did. . . . No, wait. Mom, you tell me about something naughty that Aunt Morgan did."

"Oh, you are a stinker," said my aunt.

Mom had closed her eyes. At first I thought she had suddenly dropped off to sleep, but then I realized she was thinking. "Well, there was the time she gave both of us haircuts. She told me she could make my hair look exactly like Marlo Thomas's on That Girl. Have you ever seen the reruns of that show, honey?" Mom asked me.

I nodded. Then I asked. "How old were you guys then?"

"Why, that was just last year," Dad spoke up, and we all laughed.

"No, I was about ten," said Aunt Morgan, "and your mother was about eight. Why she fell for a line like that, I'll never know."

"You were my big sister. I believed everything you said," said Mom.

"Not everything," said Aunt Morgan.

"Almost everything."

"Well, anyway, I had absolutely no idea how to give someone's hair a trim, let alone style it like Marlo Thomas's," said my aunt. "But I felt I could experiment on my little sister. I thought that if I did a good job I could open up a beauty business in our basement and style hair for all the neighborhood kids. It seemed like a gold mine."

"And what happened?" I asked.

"I wound up nearly bald — looking a lot like I do right now," said Mom.

There was this big embarrassed silence in the room and then we all started laughing again.

"Did you get in trouble, Morgan?" Dad wanted to know.

"Plenty," she replied. "Grounded, fined, the works."

"FINED?" I REPEATED.

"MY ALLOWANCE WAS DOCKED. THAT WAS WHAT OUR PARENTS CALLED BEING FINED."

MOM SMILED WANLY AT THAT. "MORGAN GOT FINED A LOT MORE OFTEN THAN I DID," SHE SAID WEAKLY.

I LOOKED AT MY WATCH. WE'D ONLY BEEN TALKING FOR FIFTEEN MINUTES OR SO, BUT I WAS PRETTY SURE THAT ALREADY THAT INJECTION WAS WEARING OFF. I LOOKED HELPLESSLY AT MY AUNT. I THINK SHE KNEW WHAT I WAS THINKING, WHICH WAS, CAN MOM HAVE ANOTHER INJECTION NOW?

AUNT MORGAN SHOOK HER HEAD SLIGHTLY.

THEN I HAD A THOUGHT. I REMEMBERED WHAT DAD HAD SAID AT DINNER.

"MOM, DO YOU WANT TO WRITE ANYTHING DOWN?" I ASKED HER.

MOM COULDN'T ANSWER. SHE STARTED TO COUGH.

DAD LURCHED FOR THE BED AND I JUMPED ASIDE TO GIVE HIM ROOM. HE SAT WITH HER, HOLDING HER GENTLY UNTIL THE COUGHING STOPPED.

MOM IS HAVING A REALLY BAD MORNING. I WONDER WHETHER SHE CAN HOLD OUT FOR TWO MORE DAYS. I WONDER WHETHER SHE CAN EVEN LAST UNTIL THE END OF THIS DAY. A NURSE AND THE DOCTOR ARE DOWNSTAIRS RIGHT NOW, AND THEY'RE IN MOM'S ROOM, ALONG WITH DAD AND AUNT MORGAN. I PEEKED IN A WHILE AGO, BUT NO ONE NOTICED ME. MOM SEEMED AWFULLY GROGGY, SO I'M BACK UP HERE.

LAST NIGHT, AFTER THE COUGHING STOPPED, DAD AND AUNT MORGAN AND I SAT WITH MOM UNTIL SHE FELL ASLEEP. THEN WE TIPTOED INTO THE LIVING ROOM AND SAT THERE FOR A LONG TIME. I AM LOOKING AT AUNT MORGAN WITH NEW EYES. SO SHE WAS A TROUBLEMAKER WHEN SHE WAS A KID. AND SHE HAD A SENSE OF HUMOR. I'D NEVER HAVE GUESSED IT. SHE SEEMS SO STODGY AND STIFF AND CONTROLLING. THEN AGAIN, SINCE SHE LIVES IN ATLANTA AND WE'VE LIVED IN CALIFORNIA ALL MY LIFE, HOW OFTEN HAVE I SEEN HER? SIX OR SEVEN TIMES? AND TWO OF THOSE TIMES HAVE BEEN SINCE MOM GOT SICK. MAYBE THIS IS JUST HOW AUNT MORGAN DEALS WITH

STRESS. MAYBE SHE'S REALLY A VERY NICE, FUNNY PERSON AFTER ALL.

MAYBE I SHOULD GET TO KNOW HER BETTER.

9:17 A.M.

DAD KNOCKED ON MY DOOR A LITTLE WHILE AGO, AFTER THE DOCTOR LEFT.

"COME IN," I CALLED.

"SWEETIE, CAN I TALK TO YOU?" HE ASKED. HE SAT ON THE BED.

(OH, BOY. POUNDING HEART, COLD HANDS. THAT FEAR.)

"SURE," I SAID IN A TINY LITTLE VOICE.

"THE DOCTOR THINKS MOM WON'T LAST THE DAY."

I DIDN'T KNOW WHAT TO SAY. ALL I COULD THINK WAS, YESTERDAY YOU SAID SHE MIGHT HAVE THREE MORE DAYS. BUT I KNEW THAT WAS A FOOLISH, CHILDISH THOUGHT. NOBODY KNOWS ANYTHING FOR SURE, NOT EVEN THE DOCTOR. I STARED OUT MY WINDOW. AT LAST I SAID, "THEN I GUESS I SHOULD COME DOWNSTAIRS."

"WHENEVER YOU WANT." DAD PAUSED. "AND SUNNY, YOU DON'T HAVE TO COME DOWNSTAIRS. YOU

DON'T HAVE TO SEE MOM. YOU DON'T EVEN HAVE
TO SAY GOOD-BYE TO HER — ALTHOUGH I KNOW SHE
WANTS TO SAY GOOD-BYE TO YOU."

"NO, I'M COMING."

"OKAY." DAD LEFT MY ROOM.

I LOOKED AT MY JOURNAL. I WANT TO
RECORD EVERYTHING IN IT. THAT MEANS I
WANT TO HAVE IT WITH ME AT ALL TIMES. I
WONDER IF AUNT MORGAN WILL UNDERSTAND.

9:29 A.M.

I THINK SHE WILL UNDERSTAND.

10:16 A.M.

MOM IS IN THE WORST SHAPE I HAVE EVER
SEEN HER IN, AND THAT'S SAYING A LOT. SHE'S IN
SO MUCH PAIN. USUALLY WHEN THE PAIN BECOMES
TOO GREAT, SHE TRIES TO FIND A WAY TO FALL
ASLEEP, BUT NOW SHE'S TRYING TO STAY AWAKE.
SHE KEEPS THINKING OF THINGS SHE WANTS TO
TELL US, THINGS SHE WANTS TO SAY. ALSO, I
HAVE A FEELING THAT SHE DOESN'T WANT TO MISS

ANYTHING, DOESN'T WANT TO SLEEP THROUGH A
SINGLE SECOND OF THE TIME SHE HAS LEFT.

10:42 A.M.

DAD AND I ARE IN MOM'S ROOM. A FUNNY
THING. SHE JUST ASKED US TO OPEN THE CURTAINS.
IT'S A VERY BRIGHT AND SUNNY DAY TODAY, THE
KIND OF LIGHT THAT ORDINARILY HURTS MOM'S EYES.
BUT MOM SAID, "I WANT TO SEE OUTSIDE."

AT FIRST IT WAS HORRIBLE. WHEN DAD PULLED
BACK THE CURTAINS MOM HAD TO HOLD HER HANDS
OVER HER EYES. BUT VERY, VERY SLOWLY SHE
OPENED HER FINGERS A CRACK, LIKE WHEN SHE USED
TO PLAY PEEKABOO WITH ME, AND THEN VERY, VERY
SLOWLY SHE PULLED HER HANDS AWAY FROM HER
FACE. MOM COULD SEE A TREE OUTSIDE AND THE
HOUSE ACROSS THE WAY, A COUPLE OF CARS IN THE
STREET. NOT A WHOLE LOT MORE, BUT IT WAS
ENOUGH TO MAKE HER SMILE.

"I ALWAYS LOVE WHEN THE SKY TURNS THAT
COLOR," SHE MANAGED TO SAY. "THAT'S THE BEST
BLUE. THE BEST BLUE IN THE WORLD."

"DO YOU WANT ME TO CLOSE THE CURTAINS
NOW?" DAD ASKED AFTER A FEW MOMENTS.

"No. Leave them open," said Mom. But not more than ten minutes later she said weakly, "Okay, could you close them, please?" She had put her hands to her face again.

I jumped up. "I'll do it," I said.

The phone started ringing a little while ago. One call after another.

"Honey," Dad said to me, "could you be on phone duty for awhile?"

I was glad to be on phone duty. Aunt Morgan and Dad were sitting with Mom, and I wasn't sure what to do with myself. Still . . .

"What do I tell people?" I asked Dad.

He looked at me for a few moments. "The truth, honey. That she doesn't have more than a day or two."

"And what if people want to come by to see her?"

"If you think they are people she'd want to say good-bye to, then tell them to come as soon as they can, and to be prepared to stay for only a few minutes."

"WHAT ABOUT THE OTHERS?"

DAD FROWNED. "TELL THEM . . . I GUESS . . .
TELL THEM THAT WE'LL CALL THEM WHEN THERE'S
ANY NEWS."

"OKAY. I'LL KEEP A LIST OF WHO CALLS."

"THANK YOU, SUNNY."

DAD DISAPPEARED INTO MOM'S ROOM, AND NOW
I'M SITTING BY THE PHONE WITH MY JOURNAL AND
A PAD OF LEGAL PAPER. WE HAVE TWO OTHER
PADS OF PAPER GOING TOO. ONE IS A LIST OF
THINGS PEOPLE HAVE SENT — FLOWERS AND FOOD.
THE OTHER IS A LIST OF CARDS AND LETTERS.
WE'RE NOT ANSWERING THEM NOW. EVEN AUNT
MORGAN SAID WE DON'T HAVE TO DO THAT. BUT
AFTER MOM DIES WE WILL SEND A NOTE TO EACH
AND EVERY PERSON WHO WROTE TO MOM. AND WE
WILL THANK PEOPLE FOR ANYTHING THEY SENT.

11:49 A.M.

SUDDENLY THESE LISTS HAVE BECOME THE FOCUS
OF MY BEING. I AM OBSESSED WITH MAKING SURE
THEY'RE ACCURATE, COMPLETE, UP-TO-DATE. ARE THE
LISTS EASIER TO FOCUS ON THAN MOM RIGHT NOW?

SPEAKING OF <u>HIGH NOON</u>, BOY WOULD I LIKE TO WATCH AN OLD MOVIE RIGHT NOW. JUST KICK BACK WITH DAWN AND AN ENORMOUS BOWL OF POPCORN, SIT UP FOR HOURS LAUGHING AND CRYING AND IMAGINING.

12:04 P.M.

I CAN'T BELIEVE I'M FANTASIZING ABOUT WATCHING MOVIES WITH DAWN AT A TIME LIKE THIS. WHAT IS WRONG WITH ME?

12:14 P.M.

THE PHONE JUST RANG AND IT WAS REBECCA FROM MOM'S CANCER SUPPORT GROUP.

"HOW'S SHE DOING?" REBECCA ASKED ME.

I TOLD HER THE TRUTH. "NOT WELL. THE DOCTOR SAID SHE PROBABLY ONLY HAS UNTIL TODAY OR TOMORROW."

"COULD I COME SEE HER?"

A TOUGH DECISION. REBECCA IS CERTAINLY NOT

ONE OF MOM'S OLDER FRIENDS; SHE'S A VERY NEW
FRIEND. BUT SHE'S ALSO A VERY CLOSE FRIEND.

I COULD FEEL MY CHEST TIGHTENING. FIRST I
HAD TOLD DAD I WANTED THIS TELEPHONE JOB. I
HAD EVEN FELT EXCITED ABOUT IT. NOW THE SECOND
I HAD TO MAKE A TOUGH DECISION I STARTED
FEELING MAD. AND I HAD TO BE MAD AT
SOMEBODY, SO I CHOSE DAD, SINCE HE ASKED ME IF
I WANTED THE JOB.

IS REBECCA ONE OF THE PEOPLE WHO GETS
TO COME OVER OR NOT? I COULDN'T DECIDE. THEN
I THOUGHT OF A DIFFERENT QUESTION, AND
SUDDENLY EVERYTHING BECAME CLEAR TO ME AND I
STOPPED BEING MAD AT DAD. WOULD MOM WANT
TO SAY GOOD-BYE TO REBECCA? THAT WAS WHAT
DAD HAD ASKED ME TO THINK ABOUT EARLIER.

YES, I DECIDED.

"YES," I SAID TO REBECCA. "CAN YOU COME
OVER RIGHT AWAY?"

"OF COURSE."

"AND DAD SAYS VISITORS CAN ONLY STAY FOR
A FEW MINUTES."

"OKAY. I'LL BE RIGHT THERE."

I HAVE TO SAY THAT I AM KIND OF PROUD
OF MYSELF FOR HOW I AM HANDLING THIS TASK
THAT DAD TRUSTED ME WITH.

12:38 P.M.

OH GOD. ONCE AGAIN I HAVE TO ASK WHAT IS WRONG WITH ME? HOW CAN I BE THINKING ABOUT WHAT KIND OF JOB I'M DOING WHILE MOM IS IN THE NEXT ROOM DYING? THERE MUST BE SOMETHING VASTLY WRONG WITH ME. I'M SOME KIND OF ABERRATION.

12:44 P.M.

ANOTHER THOUGHT. DAD DIDN'T SAY ANYTHING ABOUT THIS, BUT THERE ARE A FEW PEOPLE I SHOULD PROBABLY CALL AND TELL TO COME OVER QUICKLY. IT WOULD BE AWFUL IF SOMEONE WANTED TO SAY GOOD-BYE TO MOM, SOMEONE MOM WOULD HAVE WANTED TO SAY GOOD-BYE TO, AND THE PERSON CALLED TOO LATE.

I STARTED A NEW LIST. PEOPLE I SHOULD CALL RIGHT NOW. I TRIED TO KEEP THE LIST AS SHORT AS POSSIBLE. AT THE TOP I WROTE DAWN AND UNDER THAT CAROL AND JACK. THEY COULD ALL STOP BY WHEN DAWN CAME HOME FROM SCHOOL. NO, THAT WON'T WORK. CAROL AND JACK WILL STILL BE AT WORK. BESIDES, WHAT IF MOM DIES while Dawn is at school? Should I call her at school? Right now? Should I call Carol and Jack at work?

This is getting out of hand.

I don't know what to do.

12:56 P.M.

What I should do is forget the stupid lists and go sit with Mom myself.

1:10 P.M.

She's getting weaker. She's hardly with us anymore. I just held her hand for a bit, then left.

1:29 P.M.

Rebecca's here. Dad let her into Mom's room, and he and Aunt Morgan and the nurse came out. They sat down in the kitchen and Aunt Morgan realized that none of us

HAD DONE ANYTHING ABOUT LUNCH. EVEN AUNT
MORGAN FORGOT THIS TIME.

"DOES ANYONE WANT LUNCH?" SHE ASKED. (A
FIRST.)

"NO," DAD AND I SAID AT THE SAME TIME.
(IT ISN'T LIKE WE NEVER EAT. THE THING IS,
PEOPLE KEEP COMING BY WITH FOOD. THERE'S STUFF
EVERYWHERE, AND WE SORT OF NIBBLE ON IT FROM
TIME TO TIME ALL DAY LONG. NOT THE MOST
HEALTHY WAY TO EAT, BUT AT LEAST WE'RE EATING.)

SO DAD AND AUNT MORGAN AND I SAT IN
THE KITCHEN AND DIDN'T SAY ANYTHING. THIS TIME,
THOUGH, THE SILENCE DIDN'T FEEL UNCOMFORTABLE.
I KNOW DAD AND AUNT MORGAN FEEL JUST THE
WAY I DO. DRAINED.

I WAS SITTING IN THE KITCHEN THINKING
ABOUT REBECCA IN MOM'S ROOM, AND OUT OF
NOWHERE I FOUND MYSELF SAYING, "I WONDER HOW
YOU SAY GOOD-BYE TO SOMEONE FOREVER."

DAD AND AUNT MORGAN LOOKED STARTLED
FOR A MOMENT, THEN THOUGHTFUL. AND THEN
THEIR EYES FILLED WITH TEARS.

"I'M SORRY," I SAID.

"NO. THAT'S OKAY." AUNT MORGAN REACHED
ACROSS THE TABLE AND PUT HER HAND ON MINE.
"I THINK WE'VE ALL BEEN WONDERING THAT."

I NODDED. "I MEAN, THIS ISN'T LIKE SAYING GOOD-BYE TO SOMEONE AT THE AIRPORT. SOMEONE YOU KNOW YOU'LL SEE AGAIN IN TWO WEEKS. OR EVEN IN TWO YEARS. THIS IS . . ."

"FOREVER," DAD FINISHED FOR ME.

"YOU KNOW," AUNT MORGAN SAID KINDLY, "I'M NOT SURE WE CAN PLAN OR PREPARE FOR SOMETHING LIKE THAT. I THINK, WHEN THE TIME COMES, THE RIGHT WORDS WILL COME AS WELL. THEY'LL JUST COME." SHE PAUSED. "AND BY 'RIGHT' I DON'T MEAN THERE ARE RIGHT OR WRONG WORDS. I MEAN THAT YOU'LL FIND THE WAY TO SAY WHAT YOU WANT TO SAY TO YOUR MOM. I TRULY BELIEVE THAT."

I WANTED TO BELIEVE THAT TOO. I DIDN'T LIKE THE IDEA OF PLANNING A SPEECH FOR MOM. I KNEW IT WOULD COME OUT SOUNDING STIFF AND FORMAL. I RELAXED A LITTLE.

1:50 P.M.

REBECCA LEFT A FEW MINUTES AGO. SHE WAS CRYING. I DIDN'T KNOW WHAT TO SAY TO HER. LUCKILY, DAD WALKED OUTSIDE WITH HER. NOW I FEEL ALL UNCOMFORTABLE. THIS IS WHAT I'M

THINKING: AFTER MOM DIES EVERYONE IS GOING TO
BE UPSET. UPSET PEOPLE ARE GOING TO DROP BY
THE HOUSE. UPSET PEOPLE ARE GOING TO PHONE
US. AND UPSET PEOPLE ARE GOING TO BE AT THE
FUNERAL. HOW AM I GOING TO DEAL WITH THEM?

1:54 P.M.

I GUESS I AM THE MOST SELF-CENTERED,
SELFISH PERSON ON THE ENTIRE PLANET. CAN I
THINK OF NO ONE BUT MYSELF?

2:10 P.M.

I SAT WITH MOM AGAIN FOR AWHILE. SHE'S
JUST SORT OF . . . DRIFTING.

2:35 P.M.

I'VE SET MYSELF UP IN MOM'S ROOM. I
DRAGGED AN ARMCHAIR IN HERE. I JAMMED IT
BETWEEN THE DOORWAY AND THE FOOT OF THE BED.
DAD SAID IT WAS OKAY. I KNOW HE MEANT IT WAS

OKAY BECAUSE IT WON'T BE FOR VERY LONG, BUT HE DIDN'T SAY THAT. ANYWAY, I MOVED A TABLE NEXT TO THE CHAIR AND PUT SOME PENS AND A CUP OF TEA ON IT. I CAN LEAVE MY JOURNAL THERE WHEN I NEED TO PUT IT DOWN. I THINK I'LL JUST STAY HERE FOR AWHILE.

DAD AND AUNT MORGAN ARE IN THE ROOM TOO. THE NURSE IS JUST OUTSIDE.

THE PHONE IS BEING ANSWERED BY CAROL. THE DOORBELL RANG NOT LONG AFTER REBECCA LEFT, AND THERE WAS CAROL. SHE HAD LEFT WORK EARLY AND SHE TURNED UP HERE, SAYING SHE WAS GOING TO DO FOR US WHATEVER NEEDED DOING. SHE DIDN'T ASK US IF WE WANTED HER TO COME OVER. SHE JUST ARRIVED, READY TO HELP.

CAROL IS WONDERFUL.

VERY QUIETLY SHE TOOK OVER THE LISTS WE'D BEEN KEEPING. AND NOW SHE'S IN THE KITCHEN, STRAIGHTENING UP THE MESS WE LET PILE UP SINCE YESTERDAY — THE FOOD PEOPLE KEEP BRINGING BY. I THINK CAROL IS GOING TO REORGANIZE THE REFRIGERATOR.

MOM IS SLEEPING NOW. SHE LOOKS KIND OF PEACEFUL.

2:49 P.M.

It's funny. Now I'm sleepy myself. I think I'll take a little nap here in the chair.

3:39 P.M.

Well. I did have a nap. What a good sleep. It was very deep. Not too long, but I feel so much better.

Carol just whispered to me that Dawn is going to come over in a few minutes.

4:45 P.M.

It was awful. Horrible. I have never seen Dawn cry in quite the way she was crying after she came out of Mom's room.

Dawn talked to Mom for about ten minutes, I guess. Carol stayed busy in the kitchen, and Dad and Aunt Morgan and I sat in the living room. When Dawn came out of Mom's room she went to the kitchen and I could hear her sobbing with Carol. I didn't

KNOW WHETHER TO GO INTO THE KITCHEN OR WHAT.
AUNT MORGAN MUST HAVE REALIZED WHAT I WAS
WONDERING ABOUT BECAUSE SHE SAID, "LET HER
TALK TO CAROL FOR A BIT, HONEY. THEN MAYBE
YOU AND DAWN CAN GO TO YOUR ROOM."

I NODDED.

BUT WHEN DAWN FINALLY CAME OUT OF THE
KITCHEN WITH CAROL, SHE LOOKED AT ME AND
BURST INTO TEARS ALL OVER AGAIN. SOMEHOW IT
JUST DIDN'T SEEM APPROPRIATE TO SAY, "DO YOU
WANT TO GO TO MY ROOM?" SO I DID WHAT
FELT RIGHT. I HELD OUT MY ARMS TO DAWN AND
WE HUGGED EACH OTHER FOR A MINUTE OR TWO.

THEN DAWN BLEW HER NOSE AND SAID, "I
BETTER GO, SUNNY. I'LL SEE YOU . . ." SHE
TRAILED OFF.

WE WERE BOTH THINKING THE SAME THING:
THAT WE PROBABLY WON'T SEE EACH OTHER AGAIN
UNTIL AFTER MOM HAS DIED.

8:19 P.M.

THE REST OF THE AFTERNOON WAS MUCH
BUSIER THAN I HAD THOUGHT IT WOULD BE. I
FIGURED I WAS JUST GOING TO COZY UP IN THAT

ARMCHAIR WITH MY JOURNAL AND WATCH OVER MOM.
BUT THEN A FEW PEOPLE CAME BY ON THEIR WAY
HOME FROM WORK. THE DELIVERYMAN FROM THE
FLOWER BASKET CAME BY THREE TIMES WITH
BOUQUETS. ANOTHER DELIVERYMAN SHOWED UP WITH
A COMPLETE DINNER THAT THE PEOPLE AT THE
BOOKSTORE HAD ARRANGED TO BE SENT OVER FOR
DAD AND AUNT MORGAN AND ME. WE FELT
TERRIBLE BECAUSE THERE WASN'T ROOM FOR IT
ANYWHERE (CAROL'S CAREFULLY REORGANIZED FRIDGE
WAS BURSTING AT THE SEAMS) AND WE SIMPLY
WEREN'T HUNGRY. SO DAD SUGGESTED THAT CAROL
TAKE IT HOME SO THE SCHAFERS COULD HAVE IT
FOR THEIR DINNER. DAWN'S FATHER ARRIVED THEN,
AND CAROL PACKED IT AND SOME OTHER FOOD INTO
TWO SHOPPING BAGS. AS THEY WERE FINISHING,
CAROL REALIZED THAT BEFORE THEY LEFT IT WOULD
BE THEIR TURN TO SAY GOOD-BYE TO MOM. SHE
BURST INTO TEARS EVEN BEFORE THEY WENT INTO
MOM'S ROOM. AND WHEN THEY CAME OUT SHE
LOOKED NEARLY AS BAD AS DAWN HAD. THEN,
WORDLESSLY, SHE AND MR. SCHAFER HUGGED FIRST
DAD, THEN ME, AND HEADED NEXT DOOR.

I SAT IN MOM'S ROOM AGAIN AND WAS ABOUT
TO OPEN MY JOURNAL WHEN I NOTICED MOM
WATCHING ME FROM HER BED. I THOUGHT THAT

SURELY SHE WOULD HAVE GONE BACK TO SLEEP, EXHAUSTED, AFTER CAROL'S VISIT, BUT IN FACT SHE LOOKED PRETTY ALERT.

"HI, SWEETIE," SHE SAID.

"HI, MOM."

"WHAT TIME IS IT? I GET SO FOGGY."

"A LITTLE BEFORE SIX," I TOLD HER.

"MORNING OR EVENING?"

"EVENING."

"OH. ARE YOU GOING TO EAT DINNER NOW?"

"WE ALREADY ATE," I REPLIED, WHICH WASN'T EXACTLY A LIE, SINCE WHILE CAROL WAS WITH MOM, DAD AND AUNT MORGAN AND I PICKED AT A FRUIT BASKET THAT HAD BEEN DELIVERED.

MOM NODDED. THEN SHE FROWNED AND TRIED TO SIT UP A LITTLE.

I HURRIED TO HER SIDE AND PUT ANOTHER PILLOW BEHIND HER BACK.

"THANKS, HONEY. SUNNY?"

"YES?"

"THERE'S SOMETHING I WANT TO TELL YOU. CAN YOU GET YOUR FATHER, PLEASE?"

MY HEART DROPPED. I ACTUALLY THOUGHT I COULD FEEL IT DROP DOWN THROUGH MY CHEST CAVITY TOWARD THE GROUND.

WAS THIS IT? WAS MOM GOING TO SAY HER

FINAL WORDS? I FELT WARM ALL OVER AND KNEW
MY FACE WAS FLUSHED.

"DAD? DAD?" I SAID, RUSHING FROM THE ROOM.

"SUNNY? WHAT IS IT?" DAD LEAPED TO HIS
FEET AND WE RAN BACK TO MOM.

"MOM WANTS YOU FOR SOMETHING," I SAID.

DAD AND I HOVERED OVER MOM'S BED AND
SHE LOOKED UP AT DAD.

"I WANT TO GIVE SUNNY THE DIARIES NOW,"
SHE WHISPERED.

"OH," SAID DAD, AND AS HE SAID THE WORD
HE LET OUT A LITTLE BREATH. I COULD SEE RELIEF
WASH OVER HIM. "YES. JUST A MINUTE."

DAD LEFT THE ROOM. WHEN HE RETURNED HE
WAS CARRYING A STACK OF SPIRAL-BOUND
NOTEBOOKS. HE HANDED THEM TO ME.

I GLANCED DOWN AT THEM. THERE WERE
TWENTY OR SO. SOME OF THEM LOOKED PRETTY
OLD AND WORN. WELL THUMBED THROUGH.

"WHAT ARE THEY?" I ASKED MOM.

"MY DIARIES," SHE WHISPERED. "I STARTED
KEEPING THEM A LONG TIME AGO. WHEN I WAS
AROUND YOUR AGE. I DIDN'T WRITE IN THEM AS
MUCH OR AS OFTEN AS YOU WRITE IN YOURS, BUT
I KEPT THEM OFF AND ON UNTIL JUST A FEW
MONTHS AGO. I WANT YOU TO HAVE THEM."

"You do?" And then I asked a question that seemed silly to me, but I had to ask it. "Do you want me to read them?"

"Of course."

"But journals are private."

"Yes, I know. But I do want you to read them, Sunny. I'm not going to be around to answer all the questions you're going to want to ask me. Questions about getting married and having babies — if that's what you want to do. Or questions about how I felt on my first day at college or how my mother and I got along or what the day of my high school graduation was like. At least you can read about those things in the diaries."

I was speechless. For a long time I didn't know what to say. Finally I just said, "Thank you."

Mom reached for my hand and held it for a moment. She smiled. Then the smile faded and she grimaced. Dad called for the nurse. And I sat in my chair with the stack of diaries in my lap.

I feel like this is my mantra — I say it so often. But . . . I am so tired.

Dad and Aunt Morgan and I are in Mom's room again. After Mom gave me the diaries she had a horrible bout with pain. One of the worst ever. She was actually screaming. She screamed so loudly that the Schafers heard her next door and Carol called to see if we needed any help. Then the nurse just gave Mom something that made her fall asleep.

So Mom is simply sleeping.

Dad and Aunt Morgan and I have decided to sleep in Mom's room tonight. We'll sleep in the chairs. It seems like the right thing to do.

Of course, tired as I am, I'm nowhere near able to fall asleep at this hour, sitting up in a chair while my mother is dying nearby. Dad and Aunt Morgan aren't asleep either. Aunt Morgan is reading the Bible, and Dad is looking through those lists and some other papers.

I think I will start a list of my own: things I want to remember to say to Mom when the time comes.

1. I love you. (I guess that goes without saying, but it's always nice to hear.)

2. I think you're beautiful. (You always tell me I'm beautiful. I don't know whether you mean it, but I like to hear you, of all people, say it.)

3. I always loved the clothes you made for me, even the ones that were kind of dorky-looking. I loved them because you took the time to make them. Not all moms do those kinds of things for their kids.

4. I love that you love animals. Not in the pet kind of way but in the wild-animal kind of way. We have never had pets and I

UNDERSTAND THAT YOU DON'T LIKE THE IDEA OF "OWNING" AN ANIMAL. AND THAT YOU ESPECIALLY DON'T LIKE ANIMALS IN CAGES.

5. I LOVED THE SCHOOL LUNCHES YOU USED TO PACK FOR ME. I LOVED THAT YOU TOOK THE TIME TO MAKE SPECIAL THINGS (NOT JUST TOSS PACKAGES OF FOOD IN THE BOX) AND THAT SOMETIMES YOU WOULD HIDE A NOTE OR A SURPRISE IN THE BOX.

6. I KNOW I HAVE BEEN DIFFICULT AND FRUSTRATING LATELY, BUT I ALSO ALWAYS KNEW THAT NO MATTER HOW IMPOSSIBLE I WAS BEING YOU STILL LOVED ME. YOU HAVE TAUGHT ME WHAT UNCONDITIONAL LOVE IS.

7. I AM SORRY THAT I HAVE BEEN DIFFICULT AND FRUSTRATING.

8. I CAN'T PROMISE THAT I WILL NEVER BE DIFFICULT OR FRUSTRATING AGAIN.

9. IF DAD EVER REMARRIES I WILL TRY TO BE NICE TO HIS NEW WIFE. I KNOW THAT DAWN HASN'T ALWAYS GOTTEN ALONG WITH CAROL, BUT I WILL TRY HARD.

10. I WILL MAKE SURE DAD FINDS SOMEONE WHO WILL BE GOOD TO HIM.

11. WHAT SHOULD I DO IF DAD FINDS SOMEONE I THINK IS NOT GOOD FOR HIM? YOU

WON'T BE HERE TO HELP ME WITH THINGS LIKE
THAT.

12. MOM, I DON'T UNDERSTAND WHY YOU HAVE
TO LEAVE ME NOW. COULDN'T WE HAVE BEEN
ALLOWED A LITTLE MORE TIME TOGETHER? MAYBE
JUST UNTIL I GRADUATE FROM HIGH SCHOOL?

13. I KNOW IT ISN'T YOUR FAULT, BUT I AM
MAD AT YOU FOR LEAVING ME. PARENTS AREN'T
SUPPOSED TO LEAVE THEIR KIDS, NOT UNTIL THE
KIDS ARE ADULTS.

14. I'M SURE I WON'T BE ABLE TO REMEMBER
TO SAY ALL THESE THINGS TO YOU, SO I REALLY
WISH YOU COULD READ THIS JOURNAL. YOU GAVE ME
YOUR DIARIES, AND I WISH I COULD GIVE YOU MINE.

9:51 P.M.

JUST HAD TO TAKE A BREATHER. MY EYES ARE
ALL TEARY. PARTLY FROM CRYING, PARTLY FROM
THE DIM LIGHT IN HERE.

15. THERE ARE LOTS OF THINGS I'D LIKE TO
GIVE YOU. I WISH I COULD GIVE YOU A CURE FOR
CANCER. I WISH I COULD GIVE YOU SOMETHING THAT
WOULD REALLY TAKE AWAY THE PAIN, NOT JUST MASK

IT LIKE THOSE INJECTIONS DO. I WISH I COULD
SOMEHOW GIVE YOU A GLIMPSE OF THE ADULT I AM
GOING TO BECOME. I WISH I COULD FIND A WAY TO
TELL YOU IF YOU WILL BE A GRANDMOTHER ONE DAY.
I WISH I COULD GIVE YOU A BIG, HUGE DIAMOND-
AND-SAPPHIRE NECKLACE. IT'S NOT THE KIND OF THING
YOU'VE EVER WANTED, BUT I'D LIKE TO GIVE YOU
SOMETHING TRULY FABULOUS. I ALSO WISH I COULD
GIVE YOU A TRIP TO GREECE AND SPAIN AND ITALY.

16. MOM, I WOULD LIKE TO SEE THOSE
COUNTRIES WITH YOU. I WISH WE COULD STAND SIDE
BY SIDE AND SEE THE MEDITERRANEAN SEA
TOGETHER FOR THE FIRST TIME.

17. I WISH I COULD CRAWL BACK IN TIME AND
KNOW YOU WHEN YOU WERE A LITTLE GIRL. I
WONDER IF WE WOULD HAVE BEEN FRIENDS.

18. HOW CAN I HATE YOU FOR DYING?

11:06 P.M.

I STOPPED THE LIST A WHILE AGO. DAD AND
AUNT MORGAN ARE MAKING A VALIANT EFFORT TO
SLEEP IN HERE. I HAVE TRIED BUT JUST CAN'T DO
IT. MAYBE LATER. I AM WRITING THIS BY
PENLIGHT. (I CAN JUST BARELY SEE.)

MOM IS ASLEEP, BUT SHE DOESN'T SEEM COMFORTABLE. SHE RUSTLES AROUND AND LETS OUT LITTLE MOANS AND WHIMPERS.

DAD IS STRETCHED OUT IN HIS CHAIR WITH HIS FEET RESTING ON THE END OF MOM'S BED. HE LOOKS LIKE HE'S ASLEEP, BUT I DON'T SEE HOW HE POSSIBLY COULD BE. AUNT MORGAN IS TRYING TO SLEEP WITH HER FEET CURLED UP UNDERNEATH HER. I KNOW SHE'S NOT ASLEEP. SHE'S RUMINATING. (THAT'S WHAT SHE TOLD ME.) SHE SAID RUMINATING SOMETIMES HELPS HER FALL ASLEEP.

FRIDAY 3/19
2:32 A.M.

I DID FALL ASLEEP. NOT SURE HOW IT HAPPENED. AND WHAT JUST WOKE ME UP? OH, MOM'S AWAKE (I THINK).

2:35 A.M.

THAT WAS WEIRD. I THOUGHT MOM WAS ASLEEP, BUT SHE WAS LYING IN BED WITH HER EYES OPEN. IN THE MIDDLE OF THE NIGHT.

"Mom?" I said.

She didn't answer.

Of course I thought she had died. So I called her name again. Very softly because I didn't want to wake Dad and Aunt Morgan, who had fallen asleep after all. After a couple of seconds Mom said, "Sunny? Is that you?"

Couldn't she see me? I wondered. Well, the room was pretty dark.

"Yes, it's me."

"Oh. Okay."

And she fell asleep again.

My heart is beating really hard and my palms are sweating.

2:41 A.M.

Should I be writing all these things down? I don't know. I am chronicling my mother's death. It doesn't seem right.

But I can't be as terrible a person as I sometimes think I am, can I? I mean, I guess I could, but now I'm thinking about the things I wrote down for Mom. And I'm thinking about what a great mother she's been. If she's been such a great mother, she couldn't have raised a horrible daughter, could she have?

These thoughts are so confusing.

I wish I could ask Mom about them.

I have been dozing since the last entry. Everyone is sort of dozing now. We sleep, then wake up, then sleep a bit more. Dad seems more awake than asleep now.

I just realized something. It's another day. Mom made it through yesterday, and her doctor had thought she wouldn't. Can it be that she'll make it through today and tomorrow as well? I'm thinking of the k.d. lang song, the one about yesterday, today,

AND TOMORROW. THREE DAYS. IN THE SONG THE
THREE DAYS ARE UNBEARABLE. BUT THEY'RE ALL I
WISH FOR MOM. I WONDER. WILL SHE HAVE HER
THREE DAYS AFTER ALL?

6:55 A.M.

OH GOD. MOM STARTED BARFING A LITTLE
WHILE AGO. SHE HAS NOTHING AT ALL IN HER
STOMACH. HOW CAN SHE BARF? IT HURTS HER SO
MUCH. IT'S LIKE WHEN SHE WAS GETTING THE
CHEMO. IT'S MAKING HER CRY.

I DON'T KNOW IF I SHOULD WISH FOR THOSE
THREE DAYS FOR HER. MAYBE THAT ISN'T FAIR.
MAYBE IT REALLY WOULD BE BETTER IF SHE DIED.

6:57 A.M.

I CAN'T BELIEVE I WROTE THAT.

7:30 A.M.

CAROL JUST CALLED TO SEE HOW WE'RE DOING AND TO FIND OUT HOW MOM IS FEELING. THEN SHE SAID SHE HAS DECIDED NOT TO GO INTO WORK TODAY. SHE'S GOING TO COME OVER AGAIN AND TAKE CARE OF THINGS FOR US.

I REMEMBER THAT SHE HAS ALREADY SAID GOOD-BYE TO MOM.

8:10 A.M.

CAROL IS HERE. SHE'S FIELDING PHONE CALLS AND THE DOORBELL. DAD AND AUNT MORGAN AND I ARE CAMPED OUT IN MOM'S ROOM AGAIN. MOM FELL ASLEEP ABOUT AN HOUR AGO AND SEEMS TO BE IN LESS PAIN. THE DOCTOR WILL BE HERE SOON.

9:05 A.M.

THE DOCTOR JUST LEFT. HE SAID MOM DOESN'T HAVE MUCH TIME LEFT. OF COURSE,

YESTERDAY HE SAID HE DIDN'T THINK SHE'D LIVE
UNTIL THE END OF THE DAY AND SHE'S STILL HERE.
     I DON'T KNOW WHAT TO THINK.

                              10:24 A.M.
     I'VE JUST HAD AN IDEA. MAYBE MOM CAN'T
READ MY DIARY, BUT I COULD READ IT TO HER. I
COULD READ MY LIST OF THINGS I WANT TO TELL
HER, SO THAT I DON'T FORGET ANY OF THEM.
WHY NOT?

                              10:30 A.M.
     NOW I KNOW WHY NOT. I ASKED MOM IF I
COULD READ SOMETHING TO HER.
     "OF COURSE, HONEY," SHE WHISPERED.
     SO I OPENED THE JOURNAL TO THE LIST. I
READ ITEMS 1 AND 2, LOOKED UP, AND SAW THAT
MOM WAS ASLEEP. I DON'T KNOW IF SHE HEARD
ANYTHING AT ALL.

1:10 P.M.

Boy, this day is just dragging by. I feel like I'm sitting in a chair with a collar around my neck and someone has fastened a leash to the collar and is pulling and pulling at me and I'm not moving.

Events of the morning:

— Mom sleeping

— Dad and Aunt Morgan sitting

— Carol answering phone calls

— Two more deliveries from the florist

— Fruit basket from the fruit market

— Surprise visit from Liz, Mom's best friend from childhood, I gather, although I haven't seen Liz since I was five. Mom couldn't even wake up when Liz said her good-byes. Liz left Mom's room sobbing; Carol comforted her.

— At noon Carol insisted on fixing lunch for Dad and Aunt Morgan and me. (A few days ago, Aunt Morgan would have done that. Now she's just like Dad and me.) We all tried really, really hard to eat.

Events of the afternoon:

— None

It's happened.

It's over.

Now I'm going to try writing about it. Everything. I don't care if I have to write for hours and hours and hours. I feel as if I have nothing in my life but time. A gaping hole of time.

It started late in the afternoon. Carol was in the kitchen, Dad was in the front hallway saying good-bye to two people from the bookstore who were just leaving, and Aunt Morgan was taking a shower. (When she had said, "Maybe I'll go take a quick shower," I realized I couldn't remember when I had taken my last shower. Yesterday? The day before that?)

I was alone with Mom.

She had been asleep. Suddenly she woke up. She looked very alert, which was strange since she hadn't had an injection in quite a while. She saw me in my chair at the foot of her bed.

"Honey?" she said.

"Hi, Mom," I replied.

"Sunny, could you go get Morgan? I want to talk to her for a few minutes. Then I want to talk to you, and then I want to talk to Dad."

I thought of all those times in the last few days when something has happened to make my heart pound or my palms sweat. Now I heard these words, and I knew exactly what they meant, and . . . I felt nothing. Absolutely nothing. Just terribly, terribly calm.

"Okay," I said.

I ran from the room. I hoped Aunt Morgan was finished with her shower. If she wasn't, I thought I might have to haul her naked out of the bathroom and rush her to Mom.

I knocked on the bathroom door. "Aunt Morgan?" I called.

"Yes?"

"Aunt Morgan, Mom said she wants to talk to you. Now. And then she wants to talk to me and then to Dad."

The door flew open. Aunt Morgan stood

BEFORE ME WITH WET HAIR, BUT SHE WAS ALREADY
DRESSED, THANK GOODNESS.

"OH MY GOD. OKAY," SHE SAID.

SHE FLEW DOWN THE STAIRS AND INTO MOM'S
ROOM.

(IT JUST OCCURRED TO ME. ISN'T IT FUNNY
HOW WE SWITCHED SO QUICKLY FROM CALLING OUR
DINING ROOM "THE DINING ROOM" TO CALLING IT
"MOM'S ROOM"? IT WAS THE DINING ROOM FOR SO
MANY YEARS. WE'LL PROBABLY NEVER BE ABLE TO
THINK OF IT AS JUST THE DINING ROOM AGAIN.)

AS AUNT MORGAN RAN TO MOM, I CAUGHT
UP WITH DAD IN THE HALLWAY. HE WAS CLOSING
THE DOOR BEHIND ARLIE AND JAMES.

"DAD," I SAID BREATHLESSLY, "MOM SAID SHE
WANTS TO TALK TO EACH OF US ALONE. AUNT
MORGAN IS WITH HER NOW. THEN SHE WANTS TO
SEE ME, THEN YOU."

DAD TURNED PALE, BUT HE SIMPLY SAID,
"OKAY." AFTER A MOMENT, HE ADDED, "ARE YOU
ALL RIGHT WITH THIS, SUNNY?"

"I THINK SO."

DAD AND I SLUMPED INTO CHAIRS IN THE
LIVING ROOM AND SAT THERE WORDLESSLY, HARDLY
MOVING. A FEW MINUTES LATER AUNT MORGAN

SLIPPED OUT OF MOM'S ROOM. TEARS WERE
STREAMING DOWN HER FACE. SHE HEADED INTO THE
KITCHEN. TO BE WITH CAROL, I GUESS.

AND I STOOD UP AND WALKED INTO MOM'S
ROOM.

I SAT ON THE EDGE OF HER BED.

"HI," I SAID.

MOM SMILED AT ME.

THEN I LEANED OVER AND PUT MY ARMS
AROUND HER. I FELL AGAINST HER AND BEGAN TO
CRY. MOM STROKED MY HAIR.

"IT'S ALMOST TIME," SHE SAID TO ME.

"I KNOW." I BEGAN WILDLY TRYING TO RECALL
THE LIST I MADE. BUT I COULDN'T EVEN
REMEMBER HOW MANY THINGS I WANTED TO SAY,
LET ALONE WHAT THEY WERE. SOMETHING ABOUT
GREECE AND GETTING MARRIED AND WHEN MOM
WAS LITTLE AND WHEN I WAS LITTLE.

"I LOVE YOU, SWEETHEART," SAID MOM.

"I LOVE YOU TOO," I REPLIED. "YOU'RE THE
BEST MOTHER IN THE WHOLE WORLD."

"AND YOU'RE THE BEST DAUGHTER. I COULDN'T
HAVE ORDERED A BETTER ONE."

I TRIED TO SMILE, BUT INSTEAD I CRIED
HARDER.

MOM HELD ME AS TIGHTLY AS SHE WAS ABLE.

"You know," she said, "I'll always be with you, even if I'm not here."

"Yes."

"You and Dad — remember to take care of each other."

"Okay."

"Take care of Dawn a little too, and she'll take care of you. And go to Carol for anything. You know you can do that, don't you?"

"Yes. . . . Mom, I love you so much."

"I know." She paused. Then she said, "I love you big," just like she used to say when I was little.

I stood up. It was time to get Dad. And after Dad had his time with Mom, he and Aunt Morgan and I were going to sit with her until the very end came. We decided this, the four of us, several days ago.

I sat by myself in the living room. Aunt Morgan and Carol were still in the kitchen and I felt like being alone. Ten minutes went by. Then Dad leaned out of Mom's room and said, "Sunny, please get Aunt Morgan and come in now."

I jumped to my feet and ran to the

KITCHEN. I WAS SHAKING ALL OVER. "AUNT MORGAN," I SAID, AND I REALIZED MY VOICE WAS SHAKING TOO. "DAD SAYS TO COME IN NOW."

CAROL HURRIED TO ME AND BURIED ME IN A HUG. THEN AUNT MORGAN AND I WENT BACK TO MOM'S ROOM AND SAT ON THE BED. WE FOUND DAD NEXT TO MOM, HOLDING HER IN HIS ARMS. I SAT ON THE SIDE OF THE BED AND TOOK MOM'S HAND. AUNT MORGAN SAT AT THE FOOT OF THE BED.

IT REALLY WAS TIME.

I COULDN'T BELIEVE IT.

MOM AND DAD AND AUNT MORGAN AND I SAT ON THE BED IN SILENCE FOR A MOMENT OR TWO. THEN I TOOK AUNT MORGAN'S HAND WITH MY FREE HAND SO SHE COULD FEEL MORE CONNECTED TO MOM. FINALLY MOM SAID, "IT'S TIME."

I SQUEEZED HER HAND MORE TIGHTLY.

MOM CLOSED HER EYES. "I LOVE YOU," SHE SAID TO US. "TAKE CARE OF EACH OTHER. I LOVE YOU SO MUCH."

"I LOVE YOU TOO," DAD AND AUNT MORGAN AND I SAID.

AND THEN . . . WE ALL SAT THERE FOR NEARLY TWO HOURS. MOM'S BREATHING CHANGED. SOMETIMES SHE DIDN'T TAKE A BREATH FOR TEN OR TWENTY seconds. Her eyes became all glassy. Then, finally, they closed. I watched her chest move up and down. And then . . . I don't know what changed exactly, but it was as if I could see the fight leave her. She began to look more peaceful. More and more peaceful. Her chest was barely moving. Then it was still. For a very long time.

I started to cry.

Dad and Aunt Morgan were crying softly too.

At last Dad said, "I think she's gone."

And she was. Nobody moved for a few minutes, though.

Finally Dad stood up and cleared his throat. I ran from the room and straight into Carol's arms.

After that — it was as if the house had been asleep for a long, long time and suddenly it woke up. We made thousands of phone calls. The doctor returned. People came by.

All I could think was, What do we do now?

THIS ISN'T
HAPPENING
THIS ISN'T
HAPPENING
THIS ISN'T
HAPPENING
THIS ISN'T
HAPPENING

5:08 A.M.

WHEN AM I EVER GOING TO BE ABLE TO SLEEP AGAIN?

5:31 A.M.

IT IS SATURDAY MORNING AND MY MOTHER IS DEAD.

5:38 A.M.

THE FUNERAL WILL BE HELD ON MONDAY. MONDAY MORNING AT 11:00. DAD ARRANGED THAT LAST NIGHT. THE SERVICE WILL BE HELD AT THE PALO CITY UNITARIAN UNIVERSALIST CHURCH. I HAVEN'T BEEN THERE IN A FEW YEARS, BUT MOM AND DAD USED TO GO PRETTY OFTEN, ESPECIALLY BEFORE MOM GOT SICK. THE ONLY REASON THEY STOPPED GOING WAS BECAUSE MOM WAS IN THE HOSPITAL SO OFTEN. AND WHEN SHE WAS AT HOME SHE USUALLY DIDN'T FEEL WELL ENOUGH TO GO OUT. SHE AND DAD DID GO TO CHURCH A COUPLE OF TIMES THIS YEAR, THOUGH. AND THE MINISTER, JIM, CAME OVER TO OUR HOUSE QUITE

OFTEN. I LIKE HIM. HE ISN'T PHONY. VERY
STRAIGHTFORWARD. AND VERY OPEN. THE GOOD THING
ABOUT THE UU CHURCH IS THAT IT IS ACCEPTING OF
ALL KINDS OF PEOPLE. IT ISN'T JUDGMENTAL.

5:50 A.M.

I CAN'T BELIEVE THAT MY MOTHER IS DEAD
AND I'M ANALYZING CHURCHES.

6:00 A.M.

MOM, I MISS YOU ALREADY.

6:09 A.M.

DAD'S UP. I CAN HEAR HIM MOVING AROUND IN
HIS ROOM. HE'S CRYING. SHOULD I GO TO HIM?
I CAN'T GO TO HIM.
DAD IS IN HIS ROOM NOW. IT'S DAD'S ROOM
ONLY. IT'LL NEVER BE HIS AND MOM'S AGAIN. CAN
DAD BEAR IT?
CAN ANY OF US BEAR ANY OF THIS?

10:00 A.M.

OUR HOUSE IS LIKE GRAND CENTRAL STATION.
I WISH EVERYONE WOULD JUST GO AWAY AND LEAVE
US ALONE. WHY ARE THEY BOTHERING US?

11:10 A.M.

DAD JUST ASKED ME TO HELP OUT AND I
BLEW UP AT HIM. LIKE I USED TO DO. I'M IN MY
ROOM NOW.

EVERYBODY, LEAVE ME ALONE.

11:22 A.M.

JUST APOLOGIZED TO DAD.

I KNOW HE'S FEELING AS HORRIBLE AS I AM.

"DAD," I SAID, "I DON'T KNOW WHY I'M
ACTING LIKE THIS."

"I DO," DAD REPLIED. "BECAUSE YOU'RE MAD.
AND YOU HAVE A RIGHT TO BE."

"I DO?"

"OF COURSE."

WELL. THAT WAS NICE TO HEAR.

DAD SAT NEXT TO ME ON THE BED. "WE MAY HAVE LOST YOUR MOTHER," HE SAID, "BUT WE STILL HAVE EACH OTHER."

"I KNOW."

"WHAT MAKES YOU THE ANGRIEST OF ALL?"

I THOUGHT FOR A MOMENT. "THAT MOM PUT US IN THIS POSITION — SO THAT ALL WE DO HAVE IS EACH OTHER."

DAD GAVE ME A FUNNY HALF SMILE.

I LOOKED DOWN AT MY LAP THEN. I COULD FEEL TEARS WELLING UP IN MY EYES. FINALLY I SAID, "BUT IF ALL I DO HAVE IS ONE OTHER PERSON, I'M GLAD IT'S YOU."

DAD TOOK ME IN HIS ARMS THEN AND WE CRIED TOGETHER. IT WASN'T EMBARRASSING AT ALL. IT SEEMED QUITE NATURAL.

WHEN WE FELT A LITTLE BETTER, DAD ASKED ME AGAIN TO HELP OUT. WE NEED TO MAKE PHONE CALLS AND LOTS AND LOTS OF ARRANGEMENTS, HE SAID. HE ASKED ME IF I WOULD TALK TO THE FLORIST AND CHOOSE THE FLOWERS FOR THE FUNERAL.

TO BE HONEST, I DON'T REALLY WANT TO, BUT I SAID I WOULD.

12:07 P.M.

GOD, SOME PEOPLE ARE STUPID. DAWN WAS HERE. SHE SAID, "SUNNY, YOU SOUND SO ANGRY. WHY ARE YOU ANGRY? I THOUGHT YOU'D BE SAD." WHAT A JERK.

I JUST LOOKED AT HER AND SAID, "GET OUT OF MY ROOM."

12:22 P.M.

MyMOTHERISGONEMyMOTHERISGONEMyMOTHERISGONEMy MOTHERISGONE.

12:48 P.M.

I THINK I AM GOING CRAZY.

2:30 P.M.

CAROL HAS BEEN HERE. SHE APPEARED IN MY DOORWAY. I WAS SITTING ON MY BED. I HADN'T

CALLED THE FLORIST OR DONE ANYTHING DAD HAD ASKED ME TO DO. I'M NOT SURE WHAT CAROL WANTED TO SAY TO ME. I DIDN'T GIVE HER A CHANCE. THE SECOND I SAW HER, I STARTED TALKING. EVERYTHING JUST CAME SPEWING OUT. I SAID, "CAROL, I'M SORRY. I WAS HORRIBLE TO DAWN. I WAS HORRIBLE TO DAD. I DIDN'T MEAN ANYTHING I SAID. I WANT TO GET THE RIGHT FLOWERS. AND I WANT TO TALK TO DAWN." THEN I BURST INTO TEARS.

CAROL HELD ME AND LET ME CRY.

"YOU KNOW," SHE SAID AFTER AWHILE, "IT'S GOING TO BE A LONG TIME BEFORE YOU FEEL BETTER. THIS IS NOT GOING TO GO AWAY QUICKLY. YOU PROBABLY AREN'T GOING TO UNDERSTAND YOUR FEELINGS, OR WHAT YOU DO, OR WHAT YOU SAY. DON'T BE TOO HARD ON YOURSELF."

I NODDED, STILL CRYING.

"ON THE OTHER HAND," CAROL WENT ON, "REMEMBER THAT YOU CAN RELY ON YOUR FRIENDS AND YOUR FAMILY NOW. THEY WANT TO BE HERE FOR YOU. THEY WANT TO HELP YOU. BUT THEY MIGHT NOT ALWAYS KNOW THE BEST WAY TO HELP YOU."

"SO I PROBABLY SHOULDN'T SHOUT AT THEM," I SAID.

Carol smiled. "Well . . . not if you can help it. But that doesn't mean you can't tell people when you want to be alone. Or, if you REALLY want to shout, how about turning up your stereo full blast and screaming? You can say whatever you want. I'll tell your father that I suggested this to you."

I managed a smile. "Okay," I said.

"Now," Carol went on, "do you want me to call the florist? I'd be happy to do that."

"No. I kind of want to do it. I like the idea of choosing flowers for Mom. I don't know why I got so mad at Dad."

"Maybe you're not really mad at your father. Maybe you're just mad that the flowers have to be chosen in the first place."

3:17 P.M.

I'm spending way too much time writing in my journal.

But I have to write.

I'M EXHAUSTED. DIDN'T MENTION EARLIER WHO'S BEEN HERE TODAY. I MEAN SPECIFICALLY. IT FEELS LIKE EVERYONE ON THE PLANET HAS BEEN HERE.

GRANDMA AND GRANDAD CAME OVER LAST NIGHT, OF COURSE. AND THEY WERE HERE FOR A LONG TIME TODAY. FOR SOME REASON, I DIDN'T FEEL LIKE BEING WITH THEM. GRANDMA LOOKED HURT. SHE CALLED TO ME TWICE IN MY ROOM. FINALLY I AGREED TO EAT SUPPER WITH HER AND GRANDAD AND DAD AND AUNT MORGAN. THE FIVE OF US CROWDED AROUND THE LITTLE TABLE IN THE KITCHEN THAT WAS CRAMMED WITH FOOD AND BASKETS AND MAIL AND PACKAGES. WE TRIED TO EAT WITH ALL THIS STUFF OVERFLOWING AROUND US. OUR ELBOWS KEPT BUMPING; THERE WAS BARELY ROOM ENOUGH FOR US AND THE MEAL.

I DON'T KNOW WHAT GOT INTO ME, BUT I GAZED THROUGH THE DOORWAY INTO WHAT HAD BEEN MOM'S ROOM AND SAID, "WON'T IT BE NICE TO HAVE THE DINING ROOM BACK AGAIN? THEN WE CAN HAVE MORE SPACE."

I THOUGHT AUNT MORGAN WAS GOING TO SLAP ME. DAD BEGAN TO CRY AND LEFT THE

TABLE. SO I SLAMMED MY FORK DOWN AND LEFT
THE TABLE TOO.

It's FUNNY. I JUST REALIZED THAT I SET
OUT TO MAKE A LIST OF THE PEOPLE WHO HAVE
BEEN BY TODAY WHEN WHAT I GUESS I REALLY
WANTED TO WRITE ABOUT WAS WHAT HAPPENED AT
DINNER.

I AM A MEAN, HORRIBLE, AWFUL PERSON.

7:42 P.M.

AND I AM SO TIRED OF WRITING IN THIS
STUPID JOURNAL.

SUNDAY 3/21
7:46 P.M.

I GUESS I NEEDED A BREAK FROM THE
JOURNAL. SOMETIMES WRITING IS HELPFUL.
SOMETIMES IT INTENSIFIES EVERYTHING. I DON'T
NEED MY FEELINGS INTENSIFIED JUST NOW.

DAWN IS HERE WITH ME. SHE'S WRITING IN HER
JOURNAL TOO. IT'S BEEN SOME DAY.

Last night I apologized to Dad (again) and we all calmed down. I went to bed early and actually fell asleep. I slept for a long time — until almost 7:00 this morning.

Today was almost as busy as yesterday, but a different kind of busy. Yesterday we made the rest of the phone calls, the horrible ones when we had to tell people about Mom. Most of the funeral arrangements have been taken care of. What happened today was just that people kept coming by. In droves, it seemed. In the morning, they were mostly friends of Mom's and Dad's. After awhile I got tired of sitting with them and went to my room. A few minutes later Dawn showed up. (I told her she was brave, considering how I treated her yesterday.) She ended up staying through the afternoon. In the morning we just sat in my room and talked. Dawn is almost as sad about Mom as I am. She has her own mother, and Carol, but she was close to Mom, kind of in the way I'm close to Carol. I have to say that at first I was irritated to discover how upset Dawn was — like being upset about Mom should be my personal right since I am her actual

DAUGHTER. BUT THEN I THOUGHT ABOUT HOW I WOULD FEEL IF CAROL DIED. I GUESS IT'S OKAY FOR DAWN TO BE AS SAD AS I AM.

DAWN LOOKS HORRIBLE. PALE AND FRAGILE.

IS THAT HOW I LOOK?

AROUND LUNCHTIME, DAWN AND I CREPT INTO THE KITCHEN AND FIXED PLATES OF FOOD FOR OURSELVES. WE BROUGHT THEM BACK TO MY ROOM. WE JUST PICKED AT THEM.

"YOU KNOW WHAT?" I SAID AFTER AWHILE. "I'D KIND OF LIKE TO SEE DUCKY."

"YOU WOULD? NOW?" SAID DAWN.

"YEAH."

"WELL, LET'S CALL HIM. HE'D LIKE IT IF YOU CALLED HIM. I'M SURE HE'LL COME OVER."

SO WE CALLED HIM AND HE CAME OVER.

GOOD OLD DUCKY.

WHEN DUCKY ARRIVED ONE OF THE PEOPLE DOWNSTAIRS LET HIM IN. DAWN AND I DIDN'T HEAR THE DOORBELL RING, SO SUDDENLY DUCKY WAS JUST STANDING IN THE DOORWAY TO MY ROOM. THE SECOND DAWN AND I SAW HIM WE BURST INTO TEARS. BOTH OF US. POOR DUCKY.

DUCKY HUGGED ME FIRST, THEN DAWN. THEN HE STARTED TO CRY TOO. I THOUGHT THAT WOULD MAKE THINGS WORSE, BUT IT DIDN'T. AFTER A

MOMENT OR TWO THE THREE OF US JUST LOOKED AT ONE ANOTHER AND THEN WE STARTED TO LAUGH. AND CRY. EVERYTHING WAS ALL MIXED UP. WE WERE TRYING TO PULL OURSELVES TOGETHER A LITTLE WHEN WE HEARD SOMEONE SAY, "HI."

WE TURNED AROUND AND THERE WAS MAGGIE. IT WAS NOT LIKE HER TO DROP BY WITHOUT CALLING FIRST, SO I WAS SURPRISED. BUT MOSTLY I FOUND THAT I WAS VERY PLEASED. THERE WAS MORE HUGGING. WE WEREN'T SAYING MUCH. WE'D CRY A LITTLE, THEN SOMEONE WOULD HUG SOMEONE, THEN WE'D LAUGH A BIT.

LATER DAD CALLED UPSTAIRS, "SUNNY, TELEPHONE!"

FOR SOME REASON I CHECKED MY WATCH AS I HEADED FOR THE PHONE. I FOUND THAT HOURS HAD GONE BY. HOURS WITH MY FRIENDS, CRYING, LAUGHING, JUST BEING TOGETHER.

THE CALLER WAS AMALIA. "CAN I COME OVER?" SHE ASKED.

"YES," I SAID. "I'D LIKE THAT."

A HALF HOUR LATER AMALIA HAD JOINED DAWN, DUCKY, MAGGIE, AND ME. NOW THE FIVE OF US WERE SITTING AROUND CRYING, LAUGHING — AND TALKING A BIT MORE THAN WE HAD BEEN EARLIER.

WHEN WAS THE LAST TIME THE FIVE OF US

WERE TOGETHER IN ONE PLACE OTHER THAN SCHOOL? WAS IT THE NIGHT OF THAT DREADFUL PARTY, THE NIGHT WE MET DUCKY? THAT WAS MONTHS AGO. IT SEEMS LIKE FOREVER AGO.

I HAVE BEEN SO HORRIBLE TO MOST OF MY FRIENDS LATELY. AND HERE THEY ALL WERE, GATHERED AROUND ME LIKE A COCOON. PROTECTING ME. LOVING ME. NOT CARING HOW HORRIBLE I'VE BEEN. FOR JUST A SECOND I FELT A TEENY, TEENY BIT BETTER. THEN I REMEMBERED WHAT IS GOING TO HAPPEN TOMORROW.

PLEASE, PLEASE LET ME GET THROUGH THE FUNERAL. IT IS GOING TO BE WRETCHED. ALL I WANT IS FOR IT TO BE OVER.

8:50 P.M.

CAROL CAME UP AWHILE AGO. SHE SAT ON MY BED AND TALKED TO DAWN AND ME. DAWN WANTS TO SPEND THE NIGHT HERE. CAROL SAID IT'S OKAY. DAWN'S GOING TO THE FUNERAL TOMORROW. EVERYONE IN HER FAMILY IS GOING. CAROL HAS TOLD DAWN SHE DOES NOT HAVE TO GO TO SCHOOL AFTERWARD. DAWN WOULD BE IN NO SHAPE FOR IT.

MAGGIE, DUCKY, AND AMALIA ARE GOING TO

THE FUNERAL TOO. I WILL BE IN MY COCOON
AGAIN.

THIS AFTERNOON I ASKED DAD IF I CAN SIT
WITH MY FRIENDS DURING THE SERVICE.

"WELL," HE SAID, "FAMILY MEMBERS ARE
SUPPOSED TO SIT TOGETHER IN THE FIRST TWO
PEWS."

MY FACE MUST HAVE SHOWN MY DISMAY.
(DISMAY? IT WAS MORE LIKE SHOCK, HORROR.)

"HOW ABOUT IF WE LET DAWN SIT WITH YOU?"
HE SAID. "IF SHE DOESN'T MIND NOT SITTING WITH
HER FAMILY."

SO I TALKED TO DAWN AND CAROL ABOUT
THAT.

"IT'S UP TO YOU, HONEY," CAROL SAID TO
DAWN. "WE'D LIKE FOR YOU TO SIT WITH US, BUT
WE'LL UNDERSTAND IF YOU WANT TO SIT WITH
SUNNY."

DAWN LOOKED PAINED. I STOPPED JUST SHORT
OF SAYING TO HER, "PLEASE PLEASE
PLEASE SIT WITH ME. I NEED YOU. YOU'RE LIKE
MY SISTER. YOU HAVE TO SIT WITH ME."

MAYBE MY FACE SHOWED WHAT I WAS
THINKING, THOUGH, BECAUSE FINALLY DAWN SAID,
"OF COURSE I'LL SIT WITH YOU, SUNNY. I'LL DO

ANYTHING YOU WANT." BUT SHE SOUNDED
UNCERTAIN.

CAROL SPOKE UP THEN. "HOW MANY FUNERALS
HAVE YOU GIRLS BEEN TO?" SHE ASKED.

DAWN AND I LOOKED AT EACH OTHER. "ONE,"
SAID DAWN.

"ONE," I SAID. "MY GREAT-AUNT'S. TWO
YEARS AGO."

CAROL NODDED. "FUNERALS ARE DIFFICULT NO
MATTER WHAT, BUT WHEN YOU HAVEN'T BEEN TO
MANY . . ."

I GUESS THAT'S WHY DAWN LOOKED PAINED. IT
ISN'T JUST THAT TOMORROW IS MOM'S FUNERAL.
IT'S THE WHOLE IDEA OF A FUNERAL.

"DAWN, IF YOU WANT TO SIT WITH YOUR
FAMILY THAT'S OKAY," I SAID. (INSIDE I WAS
CRINGING.)

"NO, NO. I'LL SIT WITH YOU."

"THANK YOU," I SAID, AND LET OUT THIS
TREMENDOUS BREATH.

CAROL LOOKED AT BOTH OF US FOR A VERY
LONG TIME. "NOBODY SHOULD HAVE TO GO THROUGH
WHAT YOU'RE GOING THROUGH," SHE SAID SOFTLY,
AND TEARS CAME TO HER EYES. SHE STOOD UP.
"ALL RIGHT. I BETTER GO NOW. DAWN, ARE YOU

GOING TO COME HOME TOMORROW MORNING? OR DO
YOU WANT TO GO STRAIGHT TO THE SERVICE WITH
THE WINSLOWS?"

"I'LL COME HOME FIRST," SAID DAWN. "I NEED
TO CHANGE."

"OKAY. SEE YOU IN THE MORNING, HONEY."
CAROL KISSED DAWN ON THE TOP OF HER HEAD.
THEN SHE KISSED ME.

AND YOU KNOW WHAT? EVEN THOUGH CAROL
KISSED ME TOO, WHEN I SAW HER LEAN DOWN TO
KISS DAWN I FELT THIS HUGE KNOT OF JEALOUSY
FORM IN ME. IF CAROL HAD DIED, AND MOM WERE
SITTING HERE WITH US INSTEAD, SHE WOULD HAVE
KISSED ME FIRST.

BUT MOM IS GONE.

MONDAY 3/22
12:49 A.M.

WELL, TECHNICALLY IT IS NOW THE DAY OF
MOM'S FUNERAL. I KNOW I SHOULD BE SLEEPING.
I HAVE TRIED TO SLEEP. BUT I JUST CAN'T DO
IT. I WAS SO HOPEFUL AFTER MY GOOD SLEEP LAST
NIGHT.

DAWN AND I HAVE BEEN TALKING. TALKING
AND TALKING AND TALKING. MOSTLY ABOUT MOM.
OF ALL MY FRIENDS, DAWN KNEW HER THE BEST.
KNEW HER.
NOW I HAVE TO WRITE "KNEW" WHEN I WRITE
ABOUT MOM.

                                    12:56 A.M.
HAD TO STOP FOR A FEW MINUTES.
TEARS.
I DON'T THINK I'LL EVER GO BACK AND READ
THIS JOURNAL. I'M THINKING OF THAT SUMMER
(WHEN? TWO YEARS AGO?) WHEN I SPENT A WEEK
REREADING ALL OF MY JOURNALS. EVERY SINGLE ONE
OF THEM. IN ORDER. STARTING WITH THE VERY
FIRST ONE — SECOND GRADE AT VISTA. IF I EVER
DO THAT AGAIN, I KNOW THAT I WILL HAVE TO
SKIP THIS ONE. IT IS ACTUALLY TEARSTAINED. I
CAN'T BELIEVE I WANTED TO CHRONICLE THE END OF
MOM'S LIFE.

SIX NIGHTS AGO WHEN DAWN STARTED TO TALK
ABOUT MOM I STOPPED HER. TONIGHT, AFTER

Carol left and after Dad and Aunt Morgan went to bed, we ONLY talked about Mom. I started it.

"Remember Mom and the pennies, Dawn?" I said. "The story you started to tell last week?"

Dawn smiled. "Yeah . . . Is it all right to talk about it now?"

I nodded. "I don't think I can talk about anything BUT Mom. You know why?" (Dawn shook her head.) "I know it's ridiculous, but she's only been gone for two days and already I'm afraid I'll forget her."

"Oh, Sunny, you'll never forget her."

"What if I do?"

"Look around you. There are reminders of her everywhere." Dawn pointed to the photos of Mom, and to a vase Mom had made and the little rug she had woven. "And this is just in your room. Think of what's downstairs. Not to mention what's in photo albums and scrapbooks."

"I can't explain it," I replied. "I'm still afraid. That's why I want to talk about her."

* * *

And that's why I feel like writing about her now. I want to get everything down in this journal, even though I'll probably never read it again.

Here is the story about the pennies:

One summer day — it was VERY hot, I remember — when Dawn and I were about eight, we were bored to tears. And I think we were driving our mothers crazy. So Mom said she would take us downtown for awhile. Dawn and I were thrilled at the prospect of an adventure. Also, we thought Mom was going to buy us ice cream. So we piled into the car with our pockets full of spending money in case we also went to the toy store. To our surprise, though, after Mom had found a parking space and we started down Henry Street, Mom walked us right by both the ice cream shop and the toy store.

"Where are we going?" I asked her. Then I noticed that Mom had pulled a bag of pennies out of her purse. "What are those for?"

"Can you guess?" said Mom.

"A wishing well?" Dawn suggested.

Mom shook her head. "Nope."

"To throw in a fountain?" I said.

"Nope."

"A gumball machine?" I said hopefully.

Mom smiled. But she said "Nope" again.

Dawn and I looked at each other. We shrugged.

Then Mom opened the bag and took out a penny. Carefully she placed it heads-up on the sidewalk.

I was clueless. "What?" I said to Mom. "I don't get it."

"What does a heads-up penny mean?" asked Mom.

"Good luck," Dawn replied.

"That's right. And you can make a wish on a heads-up penny."

"But why are you leaving it there on the sidewalk?" I asked.

"So someone can find it."

At last I got the idea. "Oh!" I cried. "We're going to leave wishes for people. We can leave them all over town."

"Can we stay and watch what happens when people find the pennies?" asked Dawn.

"Sure," said Mom.

She held out the bag to Dawn and me. Each of us reached into it and withdrew a handful of pennies. Then we continued along Henry Street, setting down pennies as we went. We tried to leave them in places where we were pretty sure people would find them, but not right out in the open, because we thought they would be more fun to find if they were just a teensy bit hidden.

"Now let's get ice cream," said Mom.

She bought cones for us and we ate them on a bench outside of Krause's. From where we were sitting we could see four of our pennies.

The first two people who found them just spotted them, leaned down, picked them up, and put them in their pockets.

The third was noticed by a little girl. She was about five, just enough younger than Dawn and me so that she seemed like a REALLY little kid. I nudged Dawn and Mom. "Look," I whispered loudly.

The girl picked up the penny and tugged at her father's arm. "Daddy!" she cried. "I found a penny! And it's a good-luck penny."

"Make a wish on it," her father said.

The girl squeezed her eyes shut tightly

FOR A FEW SECONDS. WHEN SHE OPENED THEM SHE SAID, "OKAY!"

"WHAT DID YOU WISH FOR?" HER FATHER ASKED.

"OH, DADDY," SHE REPLIED. "YOU KNOW I CAN'T TELL YOU THAT. THEN IT WON'T COME TRUE. BUT IT WAS A REALLY GOOD WISH."

DAWN AND MOM AND I LOOKED AT ONE ANOTHER AND GRINNED. WE WERE ABOUT TO LEAVE WHEN WE SAW AN OLD MAN AND AN OLD WOMAN WALKING ARM IN ARM TOWARD KRAUSE'S. THE WOMAN WAS HUMMING VERY LOUDLY WHILE THE MAN SPOKE PATIENTLY TO HER.

"YOU'RE GOING TO SEE MARILYN AND THE KIDS TONIGHT, REMEMBER, DEAR?" HE WAS SAYING, AND FOR SOME REASON I HAD THE FEELING HE'D SAID IT TO HER MANY TIMES ALREADY THAT DAY.

"MARILYN?" THE WOMAN SAID VAGUELY.

"SHE'S OUR DAUGHTER," THE MAN WENT ON, AS PATIENTLY AS EVER. "OUR OLDER DAUGHTER. AND HER KIDS ARE JAMIE AND BEN."

"NOW . . . HAVE I EVER MET JAMIE AND BEN?" THE WOMAN SAID. AND THAT WAS WHEN SHE SPIED THE LAST PENNY. "OH! OH! A PENNY!" SHE CRIED.

"WHY, THAT'S THE THIRD PENNY YOU'VE FOUND TODAY," SAID THE MAN.

"Three pennies," the woman said, and she looked so happy. "Three cents. This was a three-cent walk!"

The man and the woman went into Krause's then, and I looked at Mom. "Is something wrong with that woman?" I asked her.

"I think she's just getting old," Mom replied. "Some people lose their memories when they get old."

"But she forgot who her own daughter is!" I exclaimed. I was incredulous.

Mom drew in a breath. "Well, some older people develop a disease called Alzheimer's. I think that may be what has happened to that woman."

We were silent for a moment. Then I started to grin again. "She didn't wish on the penny, but I think we made her really happy," I said. "It sounds like she has a penny collection or something. Did you see how happy we made her?"

"Yup," said Mom.

"With just a penny," said Dawn.

"Yup," said Mom again.

When Dawn and I were remembering this story tonight, Dawn said that out of all

THOSE PENNIES WE SET DOWN WE SAW ONLY ONE
PERSON, THE LITTLE GIRL, ACTUALLY MAKE A WISH.
BUT I BET WE MADE A LOT OF PEOPLE HAPPY
FOR ONE REASON OR ANOTHER. LIKE THE OLD LADY.

    AND THAT WAS ONE OF THE BEST THINGS
ABOUT MOM. SHE KNEW HOW TO MAKE PEOPLE
HAPPY. REMEMBERING THAT ABOUT HER MAKES ME
FEEL BOTH HAPPY AND SAD.

    I THINK I'LL TRY TO GO TO SLEEP NOW. MY
WRIST ACHES FROM WRITING, AND MY EYES BURN
FROM SITTING UNDER THE TINY READING LAMP.

3:13 A.M.

NO DICE.
NO SLEEP.
I DON'T WANT TO BE A ZOMBIE TOMORROW.

3:16 A.M.

ON THE OTHER HAND, WHAT DOES IT MATTER?

3:20 A.M.

GOING TO TRY AGAIN AFTER ALL.

TUESDAY 3/23
4:30 P.M.

EVERYTHING IS OVER. I NEVER EVEN WROTE IN MY JOURNAL AGAIN YESTERDAY. AND TODAY I WENT BACK TO SCHOOL. I CAN'T SAY I WAS ABLE TO CONCENTRATE. OR THAT I'LL DO ANYTHING BESIDES WRITE IN MY JOURNAL FOR THE REST OF THE DAY. BUT SUDDENLY I COULDN'T STAND SITTING AROUND THE HOUSE FOR ANOTHER MINUTE. I WANTED TO RETURN TO MY LIFE. SO I GOT UP THIS MORNING, GOT DRESSED, AND WALKED TO VISTA WITH DAWN. ALMOST LIKE USUAL.

BACK TO YESTERDAY, THOUGH.

THE DAY PASSED IN A BLUR. AT LEAST THAT'S HOW IT SEEMED AT THE TIME. BUT NOW THAT I TRY TO RECALL IT, I FIND THAT SOME DETAILS ARE COMING BACK.

DAWN AND I GOT UP EARLY. NEITHER OF US HAD SLEPT WELL, AND WE WERE VERY NERVOUS.

Dawn came out of the bathroom, sat on my bed, looked at me, and said, "Well . . . what are you going to wear?"

I couldn't believe it, but until that very second I hadn't given it a single thought.

"Oh god. I don't know," I said. "What are you going to wear?"

"I asked Carol about that yesterday and she said you don't have to wear black to funerals anymore. She said I could wear pretty much whatever I want, as long as it's, you know, sedate. I thought I'd wear my black pants and that green sweater."

"I want to wear something Mom liked," I said. And I was embarrassed to think of the horrible clothes I've been wearing lately. I'm sure Mom didn't like any of them. My torn, faded, black things. I have a lot of black, but nothing very sedate.

"What did your mom like?" asked Dawn.

I frowned and opened the closet door. "I don't know." I pawed through T-shirts and sweatshirts, leggings and hulking oversized jackets and shirts. "Stuff I used to wear last year, I guess." It took forever but finally I came up with that navy dress Mom

BOUGHT FOR ME. I HAVEN'T WORN IT VERY OFTEN AND WASN'T EVEN SURE IT WOULD FIT, BUT IT FIT WELL ENOUGH. "I GUESS THIS'LL DO," I SAID.

DAWN WENT HOME TO CHANGE, AND I WENT DOWNSTAIRS IN MY FUNERAL CLOTHES. IF DAD OR AUNT MORGAN HAD SAID ONE WORD — ONE NEGATIVE WORD — ABOUT MY OUTFIT I THINK I WOULD HAVE SCREAMED AT THEM, RUN UPSTAIRS, AND LOCKED MYSELF IN MY ROOM. BUT THEY JUST GAVE ME SAD HALF SMILES WHEN I WALKED INTO THE KITCHEN. DAD WAS SITTING AT THE TABLE DRINKING BLACK COFFEE AND WEARING HIS DARKEST SUIT AND TIE. AUNT MORGAN WAS STANDING AT THE SINK IN A BLACK DRESS WITH BLACK SHOES AND A BLACK BAND IN HER HAIR.

SO MUCH FOR NOT HAVING TO WEAR BLACK TO FUNERALS ANYMORE.

AUNT MORGAN SAID, "I CANNOT BELIEVE I AM STANDING HERE DRESSED FOR MY SISTER'S FUNERAL. THIS WASN'T SUPPOSED TO HAPPEN FOR ABOUT FORTY-FIVE MORE YEARS."

DAD'S EYES FILLED WITH TEARS AND HE STARED INTO HIS COFFEE MUG.

"OH, I'M SORRY," SAID AUNT MORGAN. SHE DISSOLVED INTO TEARS. THEN DAD DID TOO.

I LEFT THE KITCHEN.

You know what? I don't know what I did between then and the time we left for the funeral.

5:05 P.M.

Ducky just called. Checking up on me. He is a very good person.

The next thing I remember about yesterday is finding a parking space behind the church. The lot was really crowded even though we were way early, and I remember thinking, What if we're late to Mom's funeral because we couldn't find a parking space? I almost laughed. Then I almost cried. Then I concentrated on looking for a space.

"Do you think a lot of people are going to come?" I asked Dad.

"Yes," he replied grimly.

We didn't say much until we were inside. Dad found Jim (the minister) in his office and began to talk to him. Aunt Morgan and I wandered into the chapel and looked around.

"The flowers are beautiful," Aunt Morgan said. "You did a good job."

"Thank you," I replied.

We saw people gathering in the vestibule. Then Dad joined us. "We should probably go talk to everyone," he said. "Jim is going to begin the service in about fifteen minutes."

"I don't want to talk to anyone," I said.

"Then don't talk to anyone," Aunt Morgan said crossly.

She and Dad headed for the vestibule. I followed them. I felt like punching Aunt Morgan in the face.

Luckily, the first person I saw was Dawn. She was standing uncomfortably with Carol, her father, and Jeff. When she saw me, she hurried across the room and put her arms around me. Suddenly I was surrounded by my friends. Out of nowhere, Ducky, Maggie, and Amalia appeared. I was in my cocoon again. Safe.

I don't remember what we talked about.

At a few minutes after eleven, Dad touched me on the elbow. "Okay, honey," he whispered.

I GRABBED DAWN, PANICKY. "OH GOD!" I SAID, AND I KNOW I SOUNDED HYSTERICAL.

THE COCOON ENVELOPED ME ONCE MORE, LENDING ME STRENGTH. THEN DAD, AUNT MORGAN, DAWN, AND I LEFT THE VESTIBULE AND WALKED DOWN THE AISLE TO THE FIRST ROW OF PEWS. JIM LOOKED AT US FROM THE FRONT OF THE CHAPEL. HE NODDED ENCOURAGINGLY.

WE SLID INTO A PEW.

WHEN WE WERE SEATED, THE OTHER PEOPLE BEGAN TO ENTER. FIRST OUR RELATIVES, WHO SAT DIRECTLY BEHIND US. THEN OUR FRIENDS. IT REMINDED ME OF A WEDDING, AND ONCE AGAIN I WAS TEMPTED TO LAUGH, THEN TO CRY. LUCKILY, NEITHER HAPPENED.

DAWN REACHED OVER AND HELD MY HAND. DAD DID THE SAME. THEN AUNT MORGAN TOOK DAWN'S HAND. I DON'T KNOW HOW DAWN FELT ABOUT THAT, BUT IT WAS NICE FOR THE FOUR OF US TO BE LINKED.

FOR AWHILE WE JUST SAT THERE. FINALLY I WHISPERED TO DAWN, "WHEN IS IT GOING TO START?"

SHE SHRUGGED.

FIFTEEN MORE MINUTES WENT BY.

"DAD?" I SAID AT LAST. "IT'S GETTING KIND OF LATE."

"TURN AROUND AND LOOK BEHIND YOU," HE SAID.

I TURNED AROUND.

THE ENTIRE CHURCH WAS FILLED. NOT ONE SINGLE SPACE WAS EMPTY. PEOPLE WERE STANDING ALONG THE BACK, AND MORE WERE CROWDED INTO THE VESTIBULE.

JIM APPROACHED US THEN. "SORRY FOR THE DELAY," HE SAID QUIETLY. "THERE ARE PEOPLE STANDING OUT ON THE FRONT STEPS TOO, AND DOWN ON THE SIDEWALK. WE'RE TRYING TO RIG SOMETHING UP SO THAT THEY'LL BE ABLE TO HEAR THE SERVICE OUTSIDE."

I STILL CAN'T BELIEVE IT.

MY MOTHER TOUCHED SO MANY PEOPLE.

THEY LOVED HER AND SHE LOVED THEM.

WHEN JIM STEPPED AWAY, AUNT MORGAN STARTED TO CRY AGAIN. I WANTED TO CRY TOO, BUT I JUST REFUSED TO BREAK DOWN IN FRONT OF THAT HUGE CROWD. I WAS NOT GOING TO DO IT.

I DIDN'T DO IT.

(MOM, THAT IS NO REFLECTION ON YOU.)

At last the service started. Dad and Mom had talked a lot about what would happen during it. Mom wanted certain music played in the background. Her friend Jake was in the choir loft, sitting on a stool with his guitar, next to his wife, Nina, at the organ.

First they played some music that I thought might be Chopin. Then they played "Sheep May Safely Graze." I know that for sure because it was a piece of music that Mom requested over and over at the hospital.

Then they began to play "Amazing Grace." They played it through once, and then a clear, sweet voice rang out from the choir loft. I turned around to look. It was Liz. She managed to sing the entire song without crying, although just about everyone else in the church was teary-eyed by the time she finished.

After that Jake and Nina played very, very softly throughout the rest of the service. All Mom had wanted after the music ended was for people to have a chance to talk about her and remember her. Jim spoke first. He talked about the first time he met Mom. She was pregnant with me then, and he

DESCRIBED HER AS RADIANTLY HAPPY ABOUT THE
BABY SHE WAS ABOUT TO HAVE.

WHAT HAPPENED NEXT WAS HORRIBLE, AS FAR
AS I WAS CONCERNED. NO ONE ELSE, INCLUDING
DAD, SEEMED TO THINK ANYTHING OF IT, BUT I
WAS MORTIFIED. AFTER JIM FINISHED SPEAKING, DAD
STEPPED UP TO THE MICROPHONE. HE BEGAN TO
TALK ABOUT MOM. HE TALKED ABOUT HOW THEY
MET WHEN THEY WERE IN COLLEGE, AND HOW THEY
WERE DRAWN TOGETHER BY THEIR BELIEFS — IN
PEACE AND NONVIOLENCE AND GUN CONTROL, IN
ISSUES OF EQUALITY AND TOLERANCE — AND HOW THE
ONLY BIG FIGHT THEY EVER HAD WAS OVER THE
FACT THAT MOM COULDN'T HELP BUT FEEL
INTOLERANT OF INTOLERANT PEOPLE. DAD HAD TOLD
HER THAT MADE HER A HYPOCRITE, AND MOM
REPLIED THAT SHE JUST COULDN'T FEEL ANYTHING
BUT DISGUST FOR PEOPLE WHO HATED OTHER PEOPLE
BECAUSE OF THE COLOR OF THEIR SKIN OR THEIR
RELIGION OR THE SEX OF THE PERSON THEY WANTED
TO SPEND THE REST OF THEIR LIVES WITH. AND
THAT WAS THAT.

I WAS HEARING THINGS ABOUT MOM THAT
I HADN'T HEARD BEFORE. BUT THEY DIDN'T
SURPRISE ME.

ANYWAY, THE HORRIBLE THING WAS WHEN DAD

began to talk about the love that he and Mom had for each other. His voice broke and at first he simply couldn't continue speaking. But then it got worse. He began sobbing. Right up there at the microphone in front of all those people, with all those other people listening outside. I kept waiting for Jim or someone to escort him back to his seat, but no one did, and Dad seemed to want to go on. Except that he couldn't. He just stood there and cried and cried.

If I could have fit under the pew, I would have crawled there and waited until the service was over. As it was, I slid down until my head was about level with Dawn's shoulders. Aunt Morgan actually tried to haul me up, but I edged away from her.

After what seemed like hours, Dad got control of himself and continued. He talked about Mom's illness and how brave she was. He even talked about how she planned the service. All around me I could hear people sniffling and letting out little sobs.

When Dad finished, Jim hugged him hard before Dad returned to his seat. Then Dad sat down, put his head in his hands, and

BEGAN TO SOB AGAIN. I LOOKED HELPLESSLY AT DAWN. SHE SQUEEZED MY HAND, WHICH WAS HER WAY OF LETTING ME KNOW THAT I SHOULD TAKE DAD'S HAND AGAIN. SO I DID. WE SAT THAT WAY UNTIL THE SERVICE WAS OVER.

A LOT MORE PEOPLE GOT UP AND SPOKE AFTER THAT. MAYBE TEN OR EVEN FIFTEEN. NO ONE SPOKE FOR AS LONG AS DAD DID, BUT EVERYONE SAID WHAT A WONDERFUL PERSON MOM WAS, HOW SHE'LL BE MISSED, HOW SHE WAS A STAR WHOSE LIGHT HAD BEEN SNUFFED OUT, THAT SORT OF THING. THE LONGER IT WENT ON, THE LESS I FELT LIKE CRYING. I DON'T KNOW WHY. I FELT LIKE I WAS TURNING INTO A ROCK, ALL HARD AND COLD.

I COULDN'T WAIT FOR THE SERVICE TO BE OVER.

8:42 P.M.

I WANT TO FINISH WRITING ABOUT THE FUNERAL. I JUST WANT IT OUT OF THE WAY. I'VE BEEN WRITING AND WRITING AND WRITING, AND I REALLY SHOULD START TO CATCH UP WITH MY HOMEWORK, BUT I HAVE TO FINISH THIS. I'M GOING

TO WRITE IT OUT AND THEN NEVER LOOK AT IT
AGAIN. I MAY EVEN NEED TO START A NEW
JOURNAL AFTER THIS ENTRY.

WHEN THE SERVICE FINALLY ENDED, EVERYONE
FILED OUT OF THE CHAPEL. WE LEFT IN THE SAME
ORDER WE'D ENTERED. DAD AND AUNT MORGAN
AND DAWN AND I FIRST, THEN OUR RELATIVES,
THEN EVERYONE ELSE. SINCE MOM HAD BEEN
CREMATED AND THERE ISN'T GOING TO BE A BURIAL,
PEOPLE GATHERED IN THE VESTIBULE AND OUTSIDE.
THEY JUST WANTED TO TALK. OF COURSE, EVERYONE
WANTED TO TALK TO DAD AND ME. AND OF
COURSE I DIDN'T WANT TO TALK TO ANY OF THEM.
EXCEPT DAWN AND DUCKY AND MAGGIE AND
AMALIA. THANK GOD THEY FORMED THEIR COCOON
AGAIN. I LET THEM WRAP ME UP AND I WAS ABLE
TO IGNORE EVERYONE ELSE. (PRETTY MUCH.)
    I HAVE NEVER SEEN SO MUCH CRYING AND
HUGGING.
    I DON'T REALLY WANT TO WRITE ABOUT IT,
THOUGH.
    FINALLY, FINALLY, FINALLY WE WERE ABLE TO
LEAVE. DAD AND AUNT MORGAN AND I DROVE
BACK TO OUR HOUSE. I COULDN'T BELIEVE IT. THE
HOUSE WAS FULL OF PEOPLE. PEOPLE WHO HAD

BEEN AT THE FUNERAL. WHAT HAD THEY BEEN DOING THERE WHEN WE WEREN'T EVEN AT HOME YET?

IT TURNED OUT THAT THEY WERE SETTING OUT ALL THE FOOD THAT HAD BEEN DELIVERED IN THE LAST FEW DAYS, ALONG WITH STACKS OF PAPER PLATES AND CUPS AND NAPKINS (WHAT A WASTE OF TREES). A LOT OF THE PEOPLE WHO HAD BEEN AT THE SERVICE STOPPED BY THE HOUSE TO EAT AND TALK AND OFFER THEIR SHOULDERS TO DAD AND ME.

ALL I FELT WAS UNGRATEFUL AND FRUSTRATED.

I WANTED THEM OUT OF OUR HOUSE.

HADN'T THEY JUST SPENT THE MORNING CRYING AND TALKING ABOUT MOM? DAD AND AUNT MORGAN SEEMED GLAD THAT THE PEOPLE CAME BY. I WAS ONLY GLAD ABOUT MY COCOON. I DON'T KNOW IF IT WAS CORRECT FUNERAL BEHAVIOR — AND I REALLY DON'T CARE — BUT THE FIVE OF US HUDDLED UPSTAIRS IN MY ROOM AND IGNORED THE ACTIVITY DOWNSTAIRS. I DIDN'T WANT ANY KIND WORDS OR SHOULDERS UNLESS THEY BELONGED TO MY FRIENDS.

SOMEHOW THE DAY PASSED BY. ALL DURING THE AFTERNOON MY FRIENDS SAT WITH ME. AT

6:00 Amalia said she had to leave. Maggie followed soon after. Ducky and Dawn stayed until almost 10:00.

"You know what?" I said then. "I'm going to go to school tomorrow."

"Great," they replied.

And that is the end of this journal. I will never look at it again.

Part Two

Wednesday 3/24
5:58 p.m.

Brand-new journal. At least in my mind.

After I wrote the last word on the page before this one, I almost put this journal, unfinished, in the box with the others. But finally I decided that was too wasteful. So I'm starting Part Two here. I'll fold down the corner of this page so I know where the second part begins, and I'll never look at the first part again.

Went to school today. Second day back. Still can't concentrate. I wonder how long that will go on. When am I going to feel better? I known Mom's only been gone for a few days, but I've been grieving for months already. Grieving and goofing off. I'm not sure I'll be able to make up for everything I've missed this school year. I wonder if I'll have to repeat eighth grade. I've made a big mess of it.

Still, I see one good sign: I did a huge chunk of homework after school today, the

FIRST WORK I'VE DONE IN A LONG TIME. AND I SAVED WRITING IN THE JOURNAL FOR AFTER I'D DONE THE WORK.

NOW I'M GOING TO DO SOMETHING I HAD THOUGHT I MIGHT NOT DO FOR YEARS. I'M GOING TO START READING MOM'S DIARIES. I WANT TO FEEL CLOSE TO HER.

9:26 P.M.

WOW.

I'VE BEEN READING THE DIARIES SINCE DINNER ENDED. THIS IS LIKE READING SOMEONE'S AUTOBIOGRAPHY. I'M LIVING SOMEONE ELSE'S LIFE. I'M LIVING MOM'S LIFE AGAIN FOR HER.

MOM'S VERY FIRST DIARY WAS GIVEN TO HER ON HER FOURTEENTH BIRTHDAY. ALL OF HER DIARIES EXCEPT THE FIRST ONE LOOK LIKE MY JOURNALS — MESSY, WELL-WORN SPIRAL-BOUND NOTEBOOKS. BUT THE FIRST ONE, WHICH WAS A GIFT FROM HER PARENTS, IS AN ACTUAL DIARY — A SMALL BOOK WITH AN AMBER-COLORED COVER AND A BRASS CLASP THAT ACTUALLY LOCKS WITH A KEY. MOM HELPFULLY TAPED THE KEY TO THE BACK OF THE DIARY.

When I opened the diary I realized my hands were shaking a little. I was about to enter Mom's life nearly thirty years ago.

The first entry was written on the night of Mom's birthday. It starts off with:

Great birthday! Everyone was here: Janet, Liz, Molly, Dale, Nancy, Corrie, Beth. We had a swim party. Well, that was no surprise because I arranged it. But Mom and Dad didn't tell me that Aunt Mel and Uncle Rick were going to come with Caroline and Peter. Fun to see them! Peter is so cute! He's almost four now. And Caroline is so good with him. Now that she can read, she reads stories to him all the time.

Got great presents! This one is the best! I'll write in it every day!

I frowned a little as I read this entry. It seemed just the teeniest bit immature to me. Then I thought about how small the diary was, and looked at the big lines on the pages. I realized that Mom had to summarize each day in twelve lines.

I KEPT ON READING. FINALLY I FLIPPED
AHEAD AND FOUND THIS ENTRY:

OCTOBER 30

GETTING READY FOR CORRIE'S HALLOWEEN
PARTY! SHE'S GOING TO INVITE BOYS! AM I
READY FOR BOYS? I GUESS I'LL FIND OUT. I'M
GLAD THIS IS A COSTUME PARTY BECAUSE I'D BE A
LOT MORE WORRIED ABOUT WHAT TO WEAR IF I
COULDN'T GO DRESSED AS A HIPPIE. (VERY EASY
COSTUME!)

(THE REST OF THIS PAGE IS A DRAWING OF
THE PARTS OF THE HIPPIE COSTUME.)

I TURNED THE PAGE.

OCTOBER 31

VERY LATE AT NIGHT.

THE PARTY DIDN'T END UNTIL ALMOST
MIDNIGHT. I HAVE REACHED A DECISION: BOYS ARE
DISGUSTING. THEY SHOULD NOT BE ALLOWED OUT OF

THEIR CAGES UNTIL THEIR VOICES HAVE CHANGED AND
THEY CAN DRESS AND SPEAK PROPERLY.

UNLESS THEY ARE KEVIN DARCY.

SIGH.

NOTE: HALLOWEEN DOESN'T MEAN CANDY
ANYMORE. MY TRICK-OR-TREATING DAYS ARE OVER.

I READ THROUGH THE AUTUMN ENTRIES AND ON
INTO DECEMBER TO SEE WHAT MOM'S CHRISTMAS
HAD BEEN LIKE. AND I CAME TO A PAGE THAT
WAS NEARLY BLANK. IT READ:

DECEMBER 13

HIGH SCHOOL IS HORRIBLE.

IT WAS FOLLOWED BY SEVERAL BLANK PAGES.
THE NEXT ENTRY WAS ON DECEMBER 17TH AND IT
WAS ALL ABOUT CHRISTMAS. THERE WAS NO
MENTION OF WHY HIGH SCHOOL WAS HORRIBLE OR
WHAT HAD HAPPENED. I DECIDED IT WAS JUST ONE
OF THOSE SCHOOL PROBLEMS. I SKIMMED THROUGH
THE REST OF THAT DIARY AND NOTICED THAT MOM
TENDED TO SKIP DAYS IN IT ANYWAY. FINALLY I
LAID DOWN THE LEATHER DIARY AND PICKED UP THE

FIRST OF THE SPIRAL-BOUND NOTEBOOKS. IT WAS SO DIFFERENT FROM MY JOURNALS. AND SO DIFFERENT FROM THE FORMAL DIARY MOM HAD GOTTEN FOR HER BIRTHDAY. SHE HAD DOODLED IN THE JOURNAL AND PASTED DOWN LETTERS, PHOTOGRAPHS, NEWSPAPER ARTICLES, TICKET STUBS, AND SO FORTH. IT WAS REALLY A SCRAPBOOK. I PAGED THROUGH IT, FASCINATED.

ONE OF THE EARLIER DATES IN THE JOURNAL WAS OCTOBER 6TH OF MOM'S SOPHOMORE YEAR IN HIGH SCHOOL. THE ENTRY FOR THAT DATE WAS SPRAWLED ACROSS TWO PAGES AND INCLUDED A SLIGHTLY BLURRY PHOTO OF THREE GIRLS IN CHEERLEADER UNIFORMS WITH POM-POMS AND A MEGAPHONE. I STARED AT THE PHOTO UNTIL I REALIZED THAT THE GIRL ON THE RIGHT WAS MOM.

MOM?

MOM WAS A CHEERLEADER?

I COULDN'T BELIEVE IT. IT DID NOT FIT IN WITH MY IMAGE OF HER. THE HIPPIE HALLOWEEN COSTUME HAD BEEN MUCH MORE APPROPRIATE. LATER IN THE SAME JOURNAL I FOUND A PHOTO THAT LOOKED LIKE IT HAD ACTUALLY BEEN CUT OUT OF A YEARBOOK. (I WONDERED WHY, AND WHERE THE YEARBOOK WITH THE HOLE IN IT WAS TODAY.) THE PICTURE WAS IN BLACK-AND-WHITE AND WAS A

GROUP SHOT OF ABOUT 25 KIDS SITTING ON BLEACHERS UNDER A BANNER THAT READ YOUNG REPUBLICANS.

NOW I WAS TOTALLY STUMPED. CHEERLEADERS. REPUBLICANS. THIS WAS NOT MOM. SHE MUST HAVE HAD A TWIN SISTER WHO HAD BEEN FELLED BY SOME WEIRD TRAGEDY, AND THIS WAS HER WAY OF TELLING ME ABOUT HER. OR MAYBE THE GIRL IN THIS PHOTO WAS AUNT MORGAN. MOM AND AUNT MORGAN LOOKED PRETTY SIMILAR. BUT NO. I READ THE CAPTION. THE GIRL WHO LOOKED LIKE MOM WAS CLEARLY IDENTIFIED, AND SHE WAS MOM, ALL RIGHT, NOT AUNT MORGAN.

I WONDERED AGAIN WHERE THE YEARBOOK WAS. I WOULD LOVE TO GET MY HANDS ON IT.

AND NOW, I CAN'T BELIEVE IT, BUT I'LL HAVE TO STOP READING AND WRITING AND GO TO BED. IT IS SO LATE. AND I'M DETERMINED TO GO TO SCHOOL TOMORROW AND DO MY HOMEWORK AND EVERYTHING.

SO . . . MORE TOMORROW.

Thursday 3/25
7:20 P.M.

Back to Mom's journals. They are all I can think about.

By the beginning of the second journal I found myself close to the end of Mom's junior year in high school. I read the first entry.

May 16

How am I going to tell Mom and Dad? They are never going to understand. I feel like I have to CONFESS something to them, and that makes me even madder, because I know I didn't do anything wrong. But if I don't tell them they're going to find out on their own. Soon too.

I better tell them.

TOLD THEM. THEY HIT THE CEILING. BOTH OF THEM. WITH THEIR STUPID CONSERVATIVE LITTLE HAIRDOS. BANGED THEM RIGHT ON THE CEILING.

I HATE MY PARENTS.

THEY WILL NEVER UNDERSTAND ME, AND I TRY TO UNDERSTAND THEM, BUT I REALLY DON'T.

DAD JUST KEPT YELLING OVER AND OVER, "YOU'RE AN EMBARRASSMENT TO THIS FAMILY."

HE SHOULD BE GLAD I DIDN'T GET ARRESTED.

AND MOM KEPT SAYING, "PEOPLE ARE GOING TO READ ABOUT THIS IN THE NEWSPAPER?"

THEN DAD SAID, "WHAT ABOUT THE YOUNG REPUBLICANS?"

AND I HAD TO TELL HIM I HAD DROPPED OUT OVER A YEAR AGO. WHEN I WAS SUFFERING FROM TERMINAL HYPOCRISY.

THE ENTRY ENDED THERE. I TURNED THE PAGE. ON IT WAS PASTED A BRIEF NEWSPAPER ARTICLE. IT WASN'T DATED OR IDENTIFIED, BUT I WAS PRETTY SURE IT WAS FROM MOM'S LOCAL PAPER. IT WAS ABOUT A PEACE MARCH THAT MOM HAD STAGED ON HER HIGH SCHOOL CAMPUS. IT WAS VERY BRIEF (THE ARTICLE, I MEAN), BUT MOM'S

NAME WAS THE ONLY ONE MENTIONED, AND IT WAS CLEAR THAT THE MARCH HAD BEEN HER IDEA AND HAD BEEN CARRIED OUT BY HER.

I WAS PUZZLED. I STILL DIDN'T UNDERSTAND WHAT WAS GOING ON BETWEEN MOM AND HER PARENTS. I ALMOST CARRIED THE JOURNAL DOWNSTAIRS TO ASK DAD ABOUT IT BUT DECIDED I WAS ENJOYING THIS PRIVATE PROCESS OF DISCOVERING MY MOTHER.

I READ THROUGH THE ENTIRE SUMMER THAT FOLLOWED, THE SUMMER BETWEEN MOM'S JUNIOR AND SENIOR YEARS IN HIGH SCHOOL. THINGS AT HER HOME WERE NOT SIMPLE AND HAPPY. BUT THEN, I KNEW THAT THE EARLY SEVENTIES WERE NOT SIMPLE AND HAPPY. THEY WERE A TIME FOR QUESTIONING AND REDEFINING AND PROTESTING AND STANDING UP FOR WHAT YOU BELIEVED IN. IT SOUNDED AS THOUGH THAT WAS JUST WHAT MOM HAD DONE BACK THEN. IT ALSO SOUNDED AS THOUGH HER PARENTS WISHED SHE HADN'T. IT ALSO SOUNDED AS THOUGH MORGAN WISHED MOM HADN'T. OR WAS MORGAN JEALOUS OF MOM? DID MORGAN WISH SHE TOO COULD STAND UP FOR HER BELIEFS — BUT SHE WAS AFRAID TO STAND UP TO HER PARENTS FIRST?

THIS WAS FASCINATING.

I READ ON UNTIL I GOT TO MOM'S HIGH

SCHOOL GRADUATION. I WASN'T THE LEAST BIT CURIOUS ABOUT HER HOPES AND DREAMS, HER FEARS AND WORRIES ON THAT DAY. WHAT I WANTED TO KNOW WAS WHAT WAS GOING ON IN HER FAMILY. I KNEW MOM HAD CHOSEN TO ATTEND UCLA, AND NOW I HAD A FUNNY FEELING THAT WAS ENTIRELY HER CHOICE, SOMETHING HER PARENTS HAD NOT WANTED.

BOY, WAS I RIGHT. MOM'S PARENTS HAD WANTED HER TO GO TO TOWNSEND, SOME TEENY, TINY CONSERVATIVE COLLEGE IN NORTHERN CALIFORNIA, THE COLLEGE MOM'S MOTHER HAD GONE TO. IT SOUNDED MORE LIKE A FINISHING SCHOOL TO ME. MOM WOULD HAVE NONE OF IT, OF COURSE. SHE WANTED TO GO TO A BIG UNIVERSITY WHERE SHE COULD STUDY WHATEVER SHE WANTED AND MEET ALL DIFFERENT KINDS OF PEOPLE.

IN THE END, MOM HAD WON. BUT SHE HAD PAID A BIG PRICE FOR IT. HER PARENTS HADN'T ATTENDED HER HIGH SCHOOL GRADUATION. NOR HAD THEY HELPED PAY HER TUITION AT UCLA. MEANWHILE, AUNT MORGAN WAS BUSY BEING THE GOOD GIRL — FOR AWHILE. SHE HAD GONE TO TOWNSEND BUT ONLY FOR TWO YEARS. THEN SHE TOOK HERSELF AS FAR FROM CALIFORNIA AS SHE COULD GET WITHOUT LEAVING THE UNITED STATES,

AND GOT HER DEGREE AT NEW YORK UNIVERSITY.
FOR YEARS SHE WASN'T IN TOUCH WITH THE REST
OF HER FAMILY — WITH HER PARENTS BECAUSE SHE
FOUND THEM AS SMOTHERING AS MOM DID, AND
WITH MOM BECAUSE, WELL, I WASN'T SURE WHY.
JUST BECAUSE THEY LIVED SO FAR APART? OR
BECAUSE SHE RESENTED THAT MOM HAD BEEN ABLE
TO STAND UP TO THEIR PARENTS LONG BEFORE HER
BIG SISTER WAS ABLE TO?

So MOM HAD PUT HERSELF THROUGH UCLA
(WHICH WASN'T EASY, BUT SHE WAS DETERMINED), AND
THAT WAS WHERE SHE HAD MET DAD. EVENTUALLY
THEY HAD GOTTEN MARRIED — AND HER PARENTS
HAD NOT ATTENDED THE WEDDING. BUT NOW AUNT
MORGAN CAME BACK INTO THE PICTURE. MOM
WROTE HER AND ASKED IF SHE'D LIKE TO COME TO
CALIFORNIA FOR THE WEDDING.

"I KNOW IT'S A LONG TRIP," SHE HAD WRITTEN
IN HER JOURNAL, RECORDING HER CONVERSATION WITH
HER SISTER, "BUT IT WOULD MEAN A LOT IF YOU
COULD BE WITH ME ON THAT DAY. IF YOU DON'T
WANT TO COME, THOUGH, I'LL UNDERSTAND."

GUESS WHAT AUNT MORGAN HAD REPLIED. SHE
HAD SENT MOM A TELEGRAM (WHO EVER THOUGHT
TO SEND A TELEGRAM?) SAYING, "IF I'M GOING

to come all that way, you'd better let me be your maid of honor."

And that was exactly what Mom had done.

This was how Mom and Aunt Morgan had become part of each other's lives again. They had stayed in touch ever since, although they were two very different people.

Aunt Morgan's next trip to California had been to see me when I was born. But before that happened, something else took place. Something huge. Something I'd heard little bits and pieces of here and there. However, until now I had never had this setting in which to place the incident.

Oh god. It's after 10:00. Time for bed.

To be continued.

Friday 3/26
Study Hall

I've got my own journal and one of Mom's here with me. I should be concentrating on catching up, especially in science and math, but the teachers don't really care what we do

IN STUDY HALL AS LONG AS WE LOOK LIKE WE'RE
WORKING.

So BACK TO MOM.

A COUPLE OF YEARS AFTER MOM AND DAD
GOT MARRIED, AND A FEW YEARS BEFORE I WAS
BORN, MOM'S PARENTS LEFT ON A CROSS-COUNTRY
SUMMER TRIP. MOM HEARD ABOUT THIS THROUGH
AUNT MORGAN, WHO WAS OCCASIONALLY IN TOUCH
WITH THEIR PARENTS. THE TRIP WAS TO LAST FOR
OVER A MONTH. BUT ON THE THIRD DAY THEIR CAR
WAS STRUCK BY A VAN AND EVERYONE IN THE
ACCIDENT WAS KILLED.

MOM WAS DEVASTATED.

AT FIRST I COULDN'T FIGURE OUT WHY. SHE
WASN'T CLOSE TO HER PARENTS, HADN'T SPOKEN TO
THEM IN YEARS. IT HAD SOUNDED AS THOUGH SHE
HATED THEM. BUT I CONTINUED TO READ, AND
SOON I SAW THAT EVEN THOUGH MOM HAD GROWN
APART FROM HER PARENTS, HADN'T UNDERSTOOD
THEM, AND KNEW THEY HADN'T UNDERSTOOD HER, SHE
STILL WANTED THEIR APPROVAL. SHE STILL WANTED
THEM IN HER LIFE. SHE HAD LONGED FOR THEM TO
ATTEND HER HIGH SCHOOL GRADUATION, HER COLLEGE
GRADUATION, AND THEN HER WEDDING. AFTER ALL
THAT TIME SHE HAD HOPED THEY MIGHT RECONCILE.

"PERHAPS," MOM WROTE, "IT WILL HAPPEN IF I HAVE A BABY ONE DAY. THEIR GRANDCHILD."

AND THEN THEY DIED.

NOW I UNDERSTAND WHY MOM HAD GIVEN ME HER JOURNALS. AT A CERTAIN POINT SHE MUST HAVE REALIZED THAT SHE WASN'T GOING TO BEAT THE CANCER, THAT SHE WAS GOING TO DIE, AND THAT LIKE HER, I AM GOING TO BE UNABLE TO SHARE SOME OF THE MOST IMPORTANT OCCASIONS OF MY LIFE WITH MY MOTHER, EVEN THOUGH FOR A VERY DIFFERENT REASON.

I HAVE JUST SET DOWN THE JOURNAL I WAS IN THE MIDDLE OF. I'VE DECIDED TO GO BACK AND START OVER AGAIN WITH THE FIRST JOURNAL, TO READ MORE SLOWLY, TO SAVOR EVERY ONE OF MOM'S WORDS. I'M NO LONGER EAGER TO RUSH THROUGH HER LIFE.

LUNCHTIME
CAFETERIA

I'M SITTING HERE BY MYSELF, AND NOW I SEE DAWN, MAGGIE, AND AMALIA. I WAS GOING TO SIT ALONE, BUT THEY'RE HEADING THIS WAY, AND THAT FEELS OKAY.

NOTE: I'M ABOUT TO START MY HOMEWORK BUT WANT TO SAY THAT I THINK TODAY WENT PRETTY WELL. NOT THAT I DIDN'T THINK OF MOM EVERY OTHER SECOND. NOT THAT I DIDN'T CRY FOUR SEPARATE TIMES IN THE GIRLS' ROOM. NOT THAT I DIDN'T NEARLY BITE JILL'S STUPID HEAD OFF WHEN SHE ASKED ME IF I MISS MY MOTHER. (SHE ACTUALLY ASKED ME THAT.) BUT I GOT THROUGH THE DAY.

TIME FOR HOMEWORK.

10:39 P.M.

NEWS OF THE DAY: I HAVE THIS ENORMOUS PIT IN MY STOMACH. IT'S JUST HUGE. IT SITS THERE AND MAKES EATING DIFFICULT AND CONCENTRATING DIFFICULT AND SOMETIMES EVEN BEING NICE DIFFICULT. BUT TODAY I WAS ABLE TO IGNORE IT A LITTLE. OR TO WORK AROUND IT. OR SOMETHING. I MADE MYSELF EAT BREAKFAST BEFORE I LEFT THE HOUSE. I ALLOWED DAWN AND THE OTHERS TO SIT WITH ME AT LUNCH, INSTEAD OF INSISTING ON SITTING ALONE. AND I ATE LUNCH. NOT A HUGE

ONE, BUT ENOUGH TO GET BY ON. WHEN I HAVE
TROUBLE CONCENTRATING IN CLASS OR ON MY
HOMEWORK I JUST FORGE AHEAD. I TELL MYSELF I
CAN THINK ABOUT MOM LOTS OF TIMES DURING THE
DAY, BUT JUST NOT AT THAT MOMENT.

To BE HONEST, I FEEL LIKE THE WALKING
DEAD, BUT AT LEAST I'M WALKING. I AM NOT
GOING TO GIVE IN TO THIS FEELING. (IS IT GRIEF?
A DIFFERENT KIND OF GRIEF? IS THIS AS BAD AS
IT GETS, OR IS THERE SOMETHING WORSE?)

11:04 P.M.

I ALMOST PUT THE JOURNAL AWAY AND WENT
TO BED, BUT I CAN'T STOP THINKING ABOUT
SOMETHING. IT'S WHAT DAD AND AUNT MORGAN
WERE DISCUSSING AT DINNER TONIGHT.

SCATTERING MOM'S ASHES. IT'S SOMETHING
MOM TALKED TO DAD ABOUT LAST MONTH, AND
TOGETHER THEY PLANNED SOME KIND OF SERVICE. A
PRIVATE SERVICE WITH DAD, AUNT MORGAN, DAWN,
AND ME PRESENT. JUST THE FOUR OF US. AND
MOM'S ASHES. DAD AND AUNT MORGAN WANT TO
HAVE THE SERVICE (CEREMONY?) SOON. TOMORROW.
AUNT MORGAN WANTS TO RETURN TO ATLANTA

PRACTICALLY THE MOMENT IT'S OVER. SHE'S EAGER
TO GET BACK. (I CAN'T BELIEVE THAT A WEEK OR
SO AGO I THOUGHT SHE AND DAD MIGHT GET
MARRIED. I KNOW THAT WILL NEVER HAPPEN. THEY
ARE WAY TOO DIFFERENT. PLUS, AUNT MORGAN
HAS HER LIFE IN GEORGIA, AND DAD HAS HIS HERE
IN CALIFORNIA.)

ANYWAY, DAD AND AUNT MORGAN WANT TO
SCATTER THE ASHES TOMORROW, SO AUNT MORGAN
CAN FLY TO ATLANTA ON SUNDAY AND GO BACK
TO WORK ON MONDAY.

BUT I AM NOT READY TO SCATTER THE ASHES.
I CANNOT DO THAT TOMORROW.

I THINK I HAVE TALKED THEM INTO HAVING
THE CEREMONY ON SUNDAY. AUNT MORGAN CAN
RETURN ON MONDAY AND START WORK ON
TUESDAY.

I JUST NEED A LITTLE TIME.

AND I HAVE TO SAY THAT WHEN I ASKED IF
WE COULDN'T PLEASE PUT THIS OFF UNTIL
SUNDAY, EVEN AUNT MORGAN LOOKED RELIEVED. I
WOULD LIKE ONE NICE RESTFUL, PEACEFUL, SCHOOL-
FREE DAY TOMORROW BEFORE I FACE THE
CEREMONY.

I ACTUALLY SLEPT LATE TODAY. SLEPT UNTIL ALMOST 9:00. DAD AND AUNT MORGAN SLEPT WELL TOO. WHEN I FINALLY CAME DOWNSTAIRS, THEY HADN'T BEEN UP FOR VERY LONG. THE THREE OF US SAT AROUND THE TABLE EATING TOAST AND CEREAL, AND TALKING. WE TALKED ABOUT OUR PLANS FOR THE DAY. I SAID I WAS GOING TO DO HOMEWORK IN THE MORNING AND SEE DAWN AND DUCKY IN THE AFTERNOON. DAD SAID MAYBE HE'D BETTER GET HIMSELF OVER TO THE BOOKSTORE, FOR A FEW HOURS ANYWAY. AND THEN AUNT MORGAN SAID, "WHAT ABOUT THE WOMEN'S SHELTER?"

"WHAT WOMEN'S SHELTER?" I ASKED.

DAD AND AUNT MORGAN GLANCED AT EACH OTHER, WHICH WAS NOT A GOOD SIGN.

"WHAT WOMEN'S SHELTER?" I ASKED AGAIN.

"WELL," SAID DAD, BUT HIS VOICE TRAILED OFF.

"WE'RE GOING TO DONATE YOUR MOM'S CLOTHES AND THINGS TO A SHELTER DOWNTOWN."

"DONATE HER <u>CLOTHES</u>?" I CRIED. "NOW?"

"SUNNY," SAID DAD.

"BUT DAD, SHE'S ONLY BEEN DEAD FOR EIGHT

DAYS. WHY ARE YOU GETTING RID OF HER THINGS ALREADY?"

"SUNNY, WHY SHOULD WE KEEP THEM?" AUNT MORGAN ASKED ME.

"WHY SHOULDN'T WE? WOULD MOM WANT US TO GET RID OF EVERY LITTLE PIECE OF HER SO QUICKLY? YOU'RE MAKING IT LIKE SHE NEVER EXISTED."

"YOU KNOW THAT'S NOT TRUE," SAID DAD.

"WELL, THAT'S WHAT IT FEELS LIKE."

"BUT WE'RE GOING TO KEEP PLENTY OF REMINDERS OF MOM. WE HAVE ALL OUR PHOTOS. AND THE HOUSE IS FULL OF THINGS SHE BOUGHT OR MADE."

"WE'RE JUST GOING TO GIVE AWAY THE THINGS WE HAVE ABSOLUTELY NO USE FOR, SUCH AS HER CLOTHES," ADDED AUNT MORGAN.

"FRANKLY, SUNNY," DAD WENT ON, "SOME REMINDERS OF HER ARE A LITTLE OVERWHELMING FOR ME. I CAN SMELL YOUR MOTHER'S SCENT IN HER CLOTHES."

THAT MADE ME SIT UP STRAIGHT. I WASN'T USED TO HEARING DAD REVEAL SUCH INTIMATE, PERSONAL THINGS. BESIDES, I KNEW WHAT HE MEANT. WALKING BY MOM'S CLOSET WAS ALMOST SHOCKING. STILL . . .

"Well, what if I want some of her clothes?" I said.

"Keep whatever you like," Dad replied. "I won't give away anything you want."

"She left some of her jewelry to you," said Aunt Morgan. "Quite a bit of it, actually."

"Okay," I said. I wasn't sure what else to say because suddenly I felt very confused. Giving away Mom's things made sense — and it didn't. I wanted her clothes and jewelry — and I didn't.

I left the kitchen to think for awhile.

When I returned, Dad and Aunt Morgan were still sitting at the table, talking.

"You already called the women's shelter, didn't you?" I said.

"Yes," replied Dad.

"Without asking me?"

"Some decisions are going to be mine alone. I'm sorry, but that's the way it is. I'll include you whenever I can. But not always."

I don't know why, but that made me feel calmer.

"When are we going to take Mom's things to the shelter?" I asked.

"In a couple of weeks," said Dad. "It'll take me awhile to sort through everything."

"Do you want me to help you?"

"If you'd like to."

"Okay. But not today."

"We don't have to start today."

1:06 P.M.

Ducky just called. He wanted to know if Dawn and I want to go to a movie this afternoon. Sounds like a good idea.

8:30 P.M.

Well, it was actually a pretty good afternoon. Just like at school yesterday, I can't say that I didn't think about Mom most of the time, or that I didn't cry several times. But still, it was not a bad afternoon.

Ducky arrived in his beat-up car and Dawn and I piled in. We drove to the mall. I'm not a HUGE fan of the mall. But today it felt like a good place to spend time. It's

FULL OF DISTRACTIONS. THE MOVIE THEATER, RESTAURANTS, STORES (EVEN IF THEY'RE SORT OF BORING ONES), PEOPLE TO WATCH. DUCKY AND DAWN ARE SO GREAT. THEY CAME PREPARED WITH LISTS OF THINGS THEY NEEDED TO DO OR BUY AT THE MALL (SO WE WOULDN'T GET BORED). DUCKY NEEDED NEW SNEAKERS, DAWN HAD TO GET A KEY COPIED, DUCKY WANTED TO LOOK FOR TWO CDs FOR HIS BROTHER, DAWN SAID SHE'D OUTGROWN HER BATHING SUIT. THEY EVEN HAD A TASK FOR ME. DAWN HAD PROMISED JEFF SHE'D GET HIM THIS WATER TOY HE'D BEEN ASKING FOR, AND SHE SENT ME OFF IN SEARCH OF IT, WHICH TOOK FOREVER. BY THE TIME WE'D BEEN TO A MOVIE AND EATEN DINNER (MEXICAN FOOD FROM THE FOOD COURT) IT WAS AFTER 6:00.

"BOY," I SAID AS WE SAT AT OUR TABLE, SIPPING THE LAST OF OUR DRINKS.

"WHAT?" ASKED SUNNY.

"THE DAY WENT BY PRETTY QUICKLY. MOSTLY THEY'VE JUST BEEN DRAGGING. EVEN AT SCHOOL. THEY'VE BEEN DRAGGING FOR WEEKS. THIS ONE FELT A LITTLE MORE NORMAL."

"WELL, THAT'S GOOD," SAID DUCKY.

"I GUESS."

"WHAT DO YOU MEAN?"

"I feel guilty."

"For feeling better?"

"Well . . . yes. I mean, Mom's funeral was just five days ago. And here I am, almost having a good time. It doesn't seem quite right."

"Don't you think your mom would want you to feel better?" asked Dawn. "She wouldn't want you to feel horrible. That would make _her_ feel bad."

I squirmed. "I know. It still doesn't feel right, though."

"So . . . what are you saying?" asked Ducky.

Now I felt cross. "I don't _know_."

"Okay, okay."

"I mean, I've never been through this before."

"Neither have we," said Ducky.

"Yesterday I nearly bit Jill's head off because she asked me if I miss Mom."

"Well, that was a fairly thoughtless question," said Dawn.

I nodded. For a moment, we were quiet. At last I said, "Anyway, it's still been a pretty good day. Thanks to you guys."

10:40 P.M.

A FEW MORE THOUGHTS ABOUT TODAY.

I GUESS I'LL JUST HAVE TO TAKE THINGS AS
THEY COME, SEE WHAT HAPPENS AS TIME GOES ON.
I KNOW DAWN'S RIGHT, THAT MOM WOULDN'T WANT
ME TO FEEL BAD. BUT I'LL JUST FEEL HOWEVER I
FEEL.

I'VE BEEN THINKING ABOUT MOM'S JOURNALS,
WHAT THEY MEANT TO HER, WHAT SHE HOPED THEY
MIGHT MEAN TO ME. I THINK I'LL KEEP MY
JOURNALS FOR HER FROM NOW ON. I MEAN, JUST
IN MY HEAD. I THINK I'LL PRETEND I'M WRITING
TO MOM, SO SHE CAN PEEK IN AT MY LIFE. I'M
ONLY THIRTEEN. MOST OF MY LIFE IS AHEAD OF
ME. I CAN'T TRULY SHARE IT WITH MOM, BUT
MAYBE I CAN IMAGINE HER BESIDE ME, SHARING MY
DAYS.

AND NOW I BETTER GET READY FOR BED.
TOMORROW WE ARE GOING TO SCATTER MOM'S
ASHES. IT'S ALL DECIDED. WE'RE GOING TO LEAVE
EARLY IN THE MORNING.

AM I READY FOR THIS?

WAS I READY FOR ANYTHING THAT HAS
ALREADY HAPPENED?

I AM SO TIRED.

I FEEL LIKE A WRUNG-OUT WASHCLOTH. BUT SOMEHOW THIS ISN'T A BAD THING. I ALSO FEEL CLEANSED. OR SOMETHING. I'M NOT SURE HOW TO DESCRIBE IT.

DAWN CAME OVER AT 8:00 THIS MORNING. SHE LOOKED NERVOUS, ALMOST AS NERVOUS AS SHE'D LOOKED ON THE MORNING OF THE FUNERAL. I COULDN'T BLAME HER. SHE LOOKED LIKE I FELT.

I PULLED HER UPSTAIRS TO MY ROOM. "DAD AND AUNT MORGAN ARE PACKING A PICNIC BASKET," I WHISPERED TO HER.

"YEAH?"

"WELL, DON'T YOU THINK THAT'S A LITTLE ODD?"

"NOT REALLY. THIS IS SUPPOSED TO BE A DAY IN HONOR OF YOUR MOTHER, ISN'T IT? SHE LOVED PICNICS."

I SHRUGGED. "I GUESS." THIS WAS ANOTHER OF THOSE THINGS THAT JUST DIDN'T FEEL RIGHT.

SOON WE WERE IN THE CAR, PULLING OUT OF

OUR DRIVEWAY. DAD AND AUNT MORGAN SAT IN
THE FRONT, DAWN AND I SAT IN THE BACK. THE
PICNIC BASKET WAS BETWEEN US. AT MY FEET WAS
THE URN CONTAINING MY MOTHER'S ASHES. I STARED
AT IT FOR AWHILE. I POKED AT IT WITH THE TOE
OF MY SNEAKER. I EDGED IT AWAY FROM ME.
FINALLY, I SAID, "AUNT MORGAN, CAN YOU TAKE
THIS, PLEASE?"

AUNT MORGAN TURNED AROUND. "WHAT?"

"THAT."

I POINTED TO THE URN. I DIDN'T WANT TO
TOUCH IT WITH MY BARE HANDS.

"I'LL TAKE IT," SAID DAWN. "PUT IT OVER
HERE."

"I CAN'T."

DAWN DIDN'T SAY ANYTHING. SHE REACHED
DOWN AND PICKED UP THE URN. I SAW THAT HER
HANDS WERE SHAKING.

THE CAR WAS SILENT UNTIL WE LEFT PALO
CITY BEHIND US AND HEADED UP THE COASTLINE.
THEN DAD SAID, "YOUR MOTHER WANTED US TO
PLAY HER FAVORITE MUSIC TODAY." HE STUCK A
CASSETTE IN THE TAPE DECK. JONI MITCHELL. ONE
OF THE TAPES MOM HAD LISTENED TO OVER AND
OVER WHILE SHE WAS SICK. EVEN SO, I STILL LIKE IT.

"She wanted us to sing along," Dad continued.

I wasn't sure I'd be able to. I had to sing around a lump that had formed in my throat. Everyone else seemed to have lumps in their throats too. But one by one, we were able to join in.

When the tape ended, I said softly, "It feels like Mom is here in the car with us."

"It's a nice feeling," said Aunt Morgan.

We put on another tape.

After that one ended, no one bothered to put on another. We sat with our thoughts for awhile. I remembered other picnics and outings that Mom and Dad and I had gone on. I remembered a time when Mom's bathing suit had fallen off while we were swimming in a lake. But for some reason the memory didn't make me laugh, even though Mom and Dad and I laughed for a very long time when it happened.

At various times on the car ride I would notice that one or another of us was crying. Then we began telling stories about Mom and soon we were laughing. Then we put on another tape.

Almost three hours went by before Dad said, "We're almost there."

"A special place?" I asked.

"The place where I proposed to your mother."

When Dad said that, part of me wanted to cry, and part of me wanted to laugh. Since I had done so much crying lately, I decided to let myself laugh. And I exclaimed, "Dad, I can't believe you and Mom were so conventional! You _proposed_ to her? Like in the movies? That's so old-fashioned. It sounds like something Mom's _father_ would have done."

"It's exactly what your father did," spoke up Aunt Morgan.

"But somehow it just felt right to us," Dad said. "It was very romantic."

"How did you propose to her, Dad? Tell us everything." Mom recorded her wedding in one of her journals but not Dad's proposal.

"Let's wait until we're there and I can show you."

"Okay." Even though what Dad was going to show us would be sad, I was awfully eager to see how he had asked Mom to marry him.

DAD PULLED OFF THE HIGHWAY AT A REST STOP, AND WE PARKED IN A LOT. WE WERE PLEASED TO SEE THAT ONLY TWO OTHER CARS WERE THERE. WE UNLOADED OUR THINGS AND AUNT MORGAN WAS ABOUT TO LOCK THE CAR WHEN I SAID, "UM, DAD, THE . . ." I GESTURED TOWARD THE URN.

DAD TOOK IT AND WE WALKED THROUGH A SMALL WOODED AREA. WHEN WE STEPPED OUT OF THE TREES WE FOUND OURSELVES ON A ROCKY CLIFF ABOVE THE OCEAN. THE CLIFF WASN'T TOO STEEP, THOUGH, AND A WOODEN STAIRCASE LED TO THE BEACH BELOW, WHERE WAVES CRASHED ON MORE ROCKS.

I HEARD DAWN SUCK IN HER BREATH. "OOH. IT'S BEAUTIFUL," SHE WHISPERED.

IT WAS STUNNING. AT FIRST, NONE OF US SAID A WORD. WE JUST GAZED OUT AT THE OCEAN. FINALLY DAD SAID, "LET'S HAVE OUR PICNIC UP HERE. WE'LL GO DOWN TO THE BEACH LATER. THAT'S WHERE MOM WANTS HER ASHES SCATTERED."

"BEFORE WE EAT, WILL YOU SHOW US HOW YOU PROPOSED TO MOM?" I SAID. I JUST COULDN'T LET GO OF THAT. I WAS DYING OF CURIOSITY.

Dad smiled. "All right."

Aunt Morgan spread a blanket on the ground and she and Dawn and I sat on it.

Dad stood by the edge of the cliff. "Well," he began, "your mother was sitting here, Sunny, with her legs dangling over the edge. And I tiptoed up behind her and stuck a yellow rose in front of her. When she turned around to look at me, I said, 'Honey, there's something I want to ask you.' I think she knew what it was, but she said, 'Yes?' very seriously. And then I got down on one knee, like this —"

"Dad, you didn't!"

"Yes, I did. And I was proud of it. Then I pulled a box out of my pocket, opened it up, and showed your mother the ring inside. I said, 'Will you marry me?' And without thinking about it for even a moment, she said, 'Yes.'"

"How long did you wait before you got married?"

"Only a few days. We'd already been living together, so it wasn't a big deal, really. We came back here to get married."

That much I had suddenly figured out,

THANKS TO MOM'S JOURNALS, BUT DAWN SAID,
"BACK HERE? TO THE CLIFF?"

"YES."

"YOU MEAN YOU BROUGHT THE MINISTER AND
EVERYONE HERE?"

"RIGHT HERE," SAID AUNT MORGAN.

"OH, THAT'S RIGHT," I SAID. "YOU WERE IN
THE WEDDING. IT WAS YOUR RECONCILIATION." DAD
AND AUNT MORGAN LOOKED AT ME, AND I ADDED,
"I'VE BEEN READING MOM'S JOURNALS." I PAUSED
FOR A MOMENT. "SHE WROTE ALL ABOUT THE
WEDDING, BUT NOT ABOUT HOW YOU PROPOSED TO
HER."

"SHE WAS FUNNY ABOUT THE JOURNALS," SAID
DAD THOUGHTFULLY. "SHE ONLY WROTE IN THEM
SPORADICALLY. SHE'D GO FOR WEEKS WITHOUT
WRITING IN THEM, AND THEN SHE'D WRITE IN THEM
FURIOUSLY FOR DAYS."

"I'M STILL GETTING A PRETTY GOOD IDEA
ABOUT HER LIFE," I SAID.

DAD TOLD DAWN A LITTLE ABOUT THE
WEDDING, AND THEN WE SET OUT OUR PICNIC. I
THINK WE HAD ALL THOUGHT WE WOULDN'T BE ABLE
TO EAT, AND THEN WE ALL REALIZED WE WERE
STARVED. SO WE DUG IN. AND WE TALKED ABOUT
MOM SOME MORE.

When we finished eating, Dad looked out at the ocean. "Well," he said, "I guess we should put our things away and go down to the beach." He looked so sad that I put my arms around him for a moment. Then, wordlessly, we set everything back in the picnic basket, and Dad cradled the urn in his arms. We made our way down the wooden stairs to the sand.

We stood in a line at the water's edge. I realized I didn't know what to do, so I looked at Dad and Aunt Morgan. They looked like they didn't know what to do either.

After a moment, Dad said, "Let's just think about your mom for a bit."

So we did.

Even though I have been doing nothing but thinking about Mom practically forever, I stood on the beach then and thought about her some more.

Dad said, "Any last things anyone wants to say to her?"

Dawn whispered, "Good-bye."

Aunt Morgan murmured, "My sister. I'll see you in the next life."

I said, "I love you, Mom."

And Dad said, "Our connection can't be broken. We're together for eternity. Good-bye."

At that point, when I heard Dad's words, the tears I'd been holding in during the picnic flooded out. In a moment all four of us were crying — sobbing and hugging. When we had calmed down, Dad opened the urn, waded into the ocean, and scattered some of the ashes over it. Then he held it out to me. I did the same, followed by Aunt Morgan, and then Dawn. I noticed, though, that Dawn was careful not to empty the urn completely. With some ashes still inside, she handed it to Dad again, and he scattered the last of Mom over the Pacific Ocean. Then he turned toward the beach and we waded ashore and climbed the stairs to the top of the cliff.

On the way Dawn said to me, "Your mom told me to take care of you."

"She told me to take care of you too."

"She just wants us all to take care of each other."

I nodded.

Dad and Aunt Morgan and Dawn and I carried our things back to the car and began

THE DRIVE HOME. THIS TIME WE DIDN'T PLAY MUSIC.
WE DIDN'T EVEN TALK MUCH. AT SOME POINT
DAWN AND I FELL ASLEEP. WE SLEPT UNTIL DAD
TURNED INTO OUR DRIVEWAY.

11:12 P.M.

CAN'T SLEEP. AGAIN.
WHY? I THOUGHT I'D BE ABLE TO SLEEP.
WHEN THE FUNERAL AND TODAY'S CEREMONY
WERE OVER, I THOUGHT I'D BE ABLE SLEEP.

TUESDAY, 3/30
4:26 P.M.

SCHOOL IS SO BORING.
LIFE IS BORING.
WHAT IS WRONG WITH EVERYONE?
WHAT IS WRONG WITH ME?
AUNT MORGAN IS GONE. DAD IS BACK AT
WORK. CAME HOME TODAY TO AN EMPTY HOUSE.
YESTERDAY TOO, BUT DAWN WAS WITH ME.
I DON'T LIKE AN EMPTY HOUSE. ESPECIALLY ONE
THAT IS EMPTY BECAUSE SOMEONE DIED IN IT.

WEDNESDAY 3/31
7:40 P.M.

DAD WORKED LATE TONIGHT SO I AM ON MY OWN.

ONE THING ABOUT AN EMPTY HOUSE. YOU GET A LOT OF HOMEWORK DONE. I AM STARTING TO CATCH UP. GOT AN A ON AN ENGLISH TEST.

FRIDAY, 4/2
5:14 P.M.

MOM, I MISS YOU SO MUCH.

HOW LONG AM I GOING TO MISS YOU IN THIS WAY?

IT HURTS.

9:37 P.M.

HEY, MOM, ARE YOU HERE WITH ME? CAN YOU READ THIS? I'M WRITING IT FOR YOU, YOU KNOW.

I THINK I CAN FEEL YOU WITH ME, A LITTLE.

I STILL REALLY NEED YOU, MOM.

I MISS YOU.

I LOVE YOU.

About the Author

ANN MATTHEWS MARTIN was born on August 12, 1955. She grew up in Princeton, NJ, with her parents and her younger sister, Jane.

Although Ann used to be a teacher and then an editor of children's books, she's now a full-time writer. She gets the ideas for her books from many different places. Some are based on personal experiences. Others are based on childhood memories and feelings. Many are written about contemporary problems or events.

All of Ann's characters are made up. But some of her characters are based on real people. Sometimes Ann names her characters after people she knows; other times she chooses names she likes.

In addition to California Diaries, Ann Martin has written many other books, including the Baby-sitters Club series. She has written twelve novels for young people, including *Missing Since Monday, With You or Without You, Slam Book*, and *Just a Summer Romance*.

Ann M. Martin does not live in California, though she does visit frequently. She lives in New York with her cats, Gussie, Woody, and Willy, and her dog, Sadie. Her hobbies are reading, sewing, and needlework — especially making clothes for children.

Maggie, Diary Three

I wonder why I've waited so long to write about what happened. I guess I was trying to forget it. Well, I can't.

As we were leaving the mall, I noticed a couple kissing in front of the movie theater. The guy's back was to me, but he looked familiar. Just then he turned around and saw me staring at them.

I quickly looked away and ran to catch up with the others.

The guy was Justin. I recognized the girl. Her name was Nancy Mercado and she was a freshman at Vista.

I didn't say anything to my friends about what I saw.

I'm glad I saw Justin and Nancy together.

Now I know which Nancy is his girlfriend. That's a lot better than not knowing.

I just wish Justin didn't see me see them.

Ugh!

What's the big deal that I saw him kissing Nancy Mercado? It's a free country. It's not like he's <u>my</u> boyfriend. We're not going out anymore. We hardly even talk.

Do I feel weird because I wish I was kissing Justin? I can't even seem to talk to him, why would I want to kiss him?

I wonder if the problem is that we never really broke up. Or is it that we never really went out? Just a couple of dates. And no kissing.

Why do I feel so awful about this? Why does it hurt so much?